Silver scintillas turned bronze, turned gold. Something ahead glittered and shed light.

She crouched lower, creeping forward to see more. What was this strangeness?

There, where the water grew abruptly deeper, a marvel gleamed below the surface, embedded in the wall of the well shaft: a mosaic of turquoise and bronze and the green of old, old copper depicting a broad-bladed sword with an almost rectangular shape to its blade.

She stared, captivated by its beauty, wondering how such artistry came to be buried in the water. The light revealing the sword brightened, and she saw it wasn't truly a mosaic, but an actual weapon.

She stretched forward, reaching to touch it, maybe to grip its hilt.

Rust appeared on the edges of the blade, dark and crusted brown, flushing swiftly to scarlet, then dimming to wine red. Its glow blackened, illuminating her fingers strangely. Her hands seemed to curve, twisting her fingers into curling claws that dripped blood.

Remeya screamed.

Also by J.M. Ney-Grimm

HUNTING WILD

BLOOD BLADE
TALE TWO

J.M. NEY-GRIMM

Wild
Unicorn

ISBN-13: 978-0692449882
ISBN-10: 0692449884

Book Design by JMNG

Cover art:
"Young Victorian Girl" by Anna Yakimova / Dreamstime.com
"Olive Trees and Cloudy Sky" by Didecs / Dreamstime.com
"Spiral Stairs in Castle" by Jeroen Kins / Dreamstime.com

Interior illustration:
"Ready for Battle" by John Green
"Castle Frame" from the Dover Pictorial Archive series

To someone very dear:
I hold you close
in my thoughts
and my heart

HUNTING WILD

Horned Lord, Three in One

Gwirionedd, essence of light and breath.

The heart's blood of the king draws Gwirionedd—Our
　　　Lord—down from heaven into his beast form on
　　　earth.

Cummenos, hunter, fell and fallen.

As Cummenos, half-man, half-stag, Our Lord hunts
　　　monsters from the lands of earth and the hearts of
　　　men, chasing his prey into the bowels of hell.

The enslaved judge, Eoin.

In hell, as Eoin, Our Lord judges evil and metes out its
　　　fate.

Gwirionedd, Our Truth.

The womb's blood of the lady frees Eoin from hell,
　　　raising him into heaven to preside as Gwirionedd—
　　　Our Lord—again.

Blessed be Our Ternion Lord.

—excerpt from the Thirty Ardanes of the Gedier,
ancient law of the old believers

REMEYA STARED at the table runner, aghast.

How had the princess dared to order *this* tapestry—of all the choices in the castle chests—placed on the console table? Yet here it lay, ready for the viands that would soon feed the princess' ladies while they watched the tourney.

A forbidden piece of household linen depicting events from a forbidden religion.

That religion had once included ritual human sacrifice, drawing their god down from the sky to cleanse the earth of evil. But it now featured only the pouring of wine and the burying of bread.

The table runner was a magnificent piece of work. If only its subject were more . . . prudent.

Remeya shivered, despite the warmth of the day.

Within the tapestry, did the green leaves of the paradise tree shiver also, stirred by a breath of air unseen amidst the forest in the brocade? Would the drop of dew sliding down the rich red of the pomegranate fall to the sun-dappled flank of the rider's bay steed? Would the powerful muscles of the stallion's haunch bunch and thrust both out of the shadows and into the light?

If I look with enough reverence, will I see him? Their horned lord with the head of a stag, the body of a man, and the heart of a god? Their taboo lord, Cummenos. *Oh, will I?*

Almost, it seemed she might.

The work was that fine. The threads that vivid. The stitches that perfect. She should know. She'd plied a needle more than enough to judge. Her nose wrinkled. She hated doing fancy work.

A burst of cheering interrupted her shocked reverie.

It was a mild, breezy day in late autumn. Remeya stood at the back of the royal box, new built for King Xavo's tourney, under the shadow of its tented canopy. The resinous scent of raw larch planks mingled with a whiff of dusty grass on moving air. Nine ladies-in-waiting clustered near the front, surveying Castel Baloron's outer bailey where the knightly bouts went forward. They chattered like a flock of vivid birds.

Plump Lady Corenna, the most stylish of them, fanned herself vigorously. The closer-than-usual fit of her green and gold brocade bodice and the weight of her elaborate skirts made her hot. Remeya stifled a giggle. Corenna thought the way her tight clothing flattened her bust made her look smaller, but the excess flesh had to go somewhere, pushing up above the edge of her ruffled chemise in two rounds more conspicuous than if they'd been covered.

Tall Lady Juneya looked cool and collected in ash blue silk shot with silver thread, her gown and the chemise under it cut in the looser silhouette reminiscent of old-fashioned robes. Lady Juneya had dignity, but somehow Remeya felt more comfortable with her than with jolly Lady Corenna.

Remeya glanced down at her own garb: a pale yellow silk gown embroidered with bronze traceries, fitted enough to be fashionable, but not tight like Lady Corenna's. A strip of her cream chemise with its cream embroidery showed at the square neck. She loved how the yellow and cream set off her long chestnut hair and her brown eyes. Velvet eyes. That's what Max had said!

If it weren't for her youth, she'd seem one of the princess' ladies. And she did share many of their duties: singing to the Princess Aeliana, fetching for her, carrying messages. But Remeya was a royal fosterling, quite an honor being reared by a princess. And unexpectedly fun.

At least it had been. In the beginning.

Metal clanged on metal as two knights lunged forward in the lists. The crowd roared again.

Hurriedly, Remeya set down the lidded tureen of bisque soup—right atop the paradise tree and the glimpse of Cummenos and his steed, visible between the branches.

There. Now it just looked like a woodland glade. Who would guess that it was the sacred grove where Cummenos rested before his wild hunt?

She descended the stairs at the back of the box to receive the next dish—a compote of orange marmalade dumplings—and ferried it up.

I'll put this one over the serpent, crushed under the horse's hoof, and then all the clues will be hidden.

The sweet citrusy smell of the marmalade should be tempting her appetite. It wasn't. The compote weighed heavily in her hands, filled with enough for the bevy attending the princess. But Remeya didn't want any.

If only, if only the princess were more timid.

A spurt of temper straightened Remeya's back as she dodged Bernessa—another fosterling, one year younger than herself—bringing a flagon of chilled wine to the table.

Damn her! Timidity, hell! Maybe a little self-preservation?

Or maybe, whispered the prompt of intuition, Remeya needed to be less entangled with the princess' choices?

But she's my fostering chaperon! I should be able to rely on her!

Remeya had been enjoying herself only a moment ago.

The pennants snapped, bright in the stiff breeze. The mood of the crowd—nobles, merchants, page boys, and peasants—fizzed, merry and poised for excitement.

As was I.

She'd bounced and cheered, enjoying the newness of the stands and the royal box, erected specially for this tourney and vivid against the old, soft red stones of Castel Baloron.

She'd waved her handkercher over her head.

"Did you see? Did you see him?" she'd demanded of Bernessa, her sister fosterling. "Maximo's footwork was perfect! Amias never even saw that backhand blow till it connected!"

"What do you know of backhand blows and footwork?" retorted Bernessa. Then she grinned. "He is good, isn't he?"

Remeya had returned her attention to the lists. "I've watched the squires in the tilting yard," she answered, eyes on the two young men finishing their bout.

Both stripped off their gauntlets to shake hands, then doffed their bronze helmets to exchange the ritual peace kisses on either cheek, indicating their good will. The jousts were tests of skill, not occasions to form enmity. Here at the *tirocinium*, an exercise for the newly knighted, it was particularly important that contestants follow the correct forms.

Amias stooped for his gauntlets and helm, limped toward his pavilion. Maximo slung an arm about his defeated opponent's shoulders, shoring him up. Evidently the two were friends, not merely civil in the aftermath of victory and defeat.

I don't know all his circle anymore, she thought. She'd used to, before his father, the Cavalier Pellucon, sent Maximo away to Castel Graezon for fostering and training. Before *her* father, Warder of Baloron, sent her to the Princess Aeliana as maid-in-waiting.

It's a good thing, she decided. He used to be grubby and annoying. *And I was . . . equally grubby and . . . equally annoying.* She smothered a grin.

Maximo had delivered Amias to his men-at-arms. Then he approached the royal box and bowed.

"Your Highness"—that was to the Princess Aeliana— "my Ladies"—another bow to the matrons- and maids-in-waiting—"my victory is yours."

He smiled directly at Remeya. "May I claim my guerdon?"

Her spirits recovered. She bounced again, once, then quelled herself. She felt a grown lady, bestowing her handkercher after a champion had jousted for her. She'd better act like one.

Max received his guerdon becomingly, no hints of their childhood association lessening Remeya's dignity, and retired with another bow.

His was the last bout of the *tirocinium*. There would be an interval before all the knights gathered for the melee. The *tiros* needed rest and refreshment. The spectators did too.

Remeya craned her neck, looking for the kitchen churls. It was her job—and Bernessa's—to carry the covered platters up to the royal box.

Ah! The churls had emerged from the barbican of the inner court. She'd risen to her feet and nudged her friend. They'd descended the stairs, Remeya first to receive the bisque soup. Remeya first to re-ascend. Remeya first to see Cummenos on the table runner.

And hide him.

"What's the matter?" whispered Bernessa. "We have to serve!"

Indeed they did.

Tall Lady Juneya wanted bisque only. Petite Lady Varice preferred the dumplings. And plump Lady Corenna requested some of everything.

The princess declined all but wine. Her thin hand trembled receiving the chalice, cool and beaded with moisture.

Remeya glanced upward in surprise. Met the royal gaze.

Aeliana smiled, but her blue eyes looked sad. The line between them deepened.

Remeya repented her earlier spurt of temper.

The princess deserved only her respect. Her position was not easy. So much had changed in two years. Aeliana herself had changed. Grievously.

Remeya remembered her first encounter with royalty. Vividly.

✝

Accompanied by her father's guardsmen and their captain, she'd arrived at Castel Cincrestes two years ago, a wide-eyed thirteen-year-old, amazed at the sight of the royal stronghold. In the heat of noontide, they'd passed under the outer gatehouse into the city and ridden up the hill, winding through the cobbled streets between narrow houses of golden-toned stone. Then under the gatehouse of the castle's curtain wall and through a succession of courts, each with its own massive gatehouse and portcullis. The vast pile of the castle bulked larger and larger. Its towers loomed ever taller. She felt smaller and smaller as the king's residence enclosed her.

When she entered the echoing receiving hall, its arched ceiling soaring overhead, its tall windows letting in a flood of sunlight to gleam on the polished marble floor, she wished she could turn and flee. It was so much more formal than the rough sandstone of her home, Castel Baloron. Being passed from one groom of the chamber to another as she travelled the long galleries helped her intimidation not at all.

By the time she reached a spacious parlor where dozens of silk-gowned ladies sat on gilded chairs or clustered here and there on an elaborate carpet, she felt utterly out of place.

The last groom of the chamber in that long chain of them led her up to a young woman perched on a window seat. Jeweled pins secured her auburn curls atop her head. Golden threads glinted in flowered brocade of her gown. She seemed more resplendent than everyone and everything else. And, yet, her face was merry, with a twinkle to her deep blue eyes and a dimple at her mouth.

"Lady Remeya, I bid you welcome! Come here, child." Her voice matched her face. Friendly and warm.

All Remeya's apprehension fell from her in an instant as she took the princess' extended hand.

That auspicious meeting heralded her initial experience at court quite accurately.

The princess conducted her household informally and encouraged intimacy from her ladies-in-waiting. Her brother, the king, despite the formality of *his* household, joined his sister for many a pleasant and convivial evening.

That was then.

It had all changed a year ago.

Remeya studied the now-strained face of her mistress. Worry had banished Aeliana's happy expression long since.

"Your Highness?" Remeya dipped a curtsey.

"My thanks, child. Truly I have little hunger. Perhaps I'll desire more when I sup this eve."

Except she wouldn't. Her Highness had displayed little appetite for near on a month.

Remeya shivered, remembering her own source of worry, wondering why her fear—yes, it was fear, not worry—and that of the princess ran in parallel.

It's our king.

On the thought, trumpets blared. Remeya started, nearly spilling the wine.

"Best put the flagon aside, child."

Remeya nodded.

"It will be well."

Except it wouldn't.

She moved to the back of the box, setting the wine vessel to hide another portion of that forbidden tapestry. It shouldn't *be* forbidden. The Holy Hermit Cathal had ended the practice of ritual slayings with his martyrdom more than one thousand years ago.

The chief herald was speaking, voice projected above the susurration of the breeze.

"His Majesty, King Xavo of Istria, Lord of Ebior"—and on with all the king's titles—"declares he shall meet Lord Rollo, High Gravine of Eirdry, in the test of the joust. May the stouter champion prevail!"

Another blast from the trumpets.

The king on his massive black stallion Morke rode from behind the most magnificent pavilion.

Remeya couldn't see his face at this distance. Could not have seen it, even were she closer, since the visor of his dark helm was down. And, truly, she did not want to see his face.

The memory of it as he had received the lost falchion from her hand one year ago troubled her still, made worry into fear.

Like all the youngsters growing up in Castel Baloron, she had explored every cranny of her home. The kitchen stores were forbidden, but harmless; the deep stores, taboo and more dangerous. The tunnel below the old bailey well, on the slope where the spring emerged from the hillside, was beyond prohibition. Forgotten.

Most memories from Remeya's fifth year were blurry now in her fifteenth.

That of her first passage up the dark tunnel behind the spring remained clear.

✝

Dared by Max—today's champion, childhood's best friend—she'd scrabbled under the earthen arch in spite of her fears.

I'm big! I'm brave! she'd insisted to herself.

She hadn't been big. Many children of Baloron never risked the underearth challenge. Those who did were nine, more often ten. But Remeya hated being the littlest, the most timid, the one causing her older companions to exercise prudence.

This would show them!

The pebbles of the underground stream bed dug into the soles of her feet, and the chill of the shallow water numbed her toes.

The rough surface of the ceiling sloped down, scraping her back, forcing her to bend, to crouch, to curl enough that she caught her balance with her hands in the wet.

The light faded swiftly. Had she gone far enough?

She paused, eyes adjusting.

The glimmering ripples of the spring's source cast dim flickers against the rocks pressing her down.

I can see.

She hesitated a moment, then moved forward, picking her way. One foot, one hand, the other foot. The roof lowered again, and her knee splashed down.

This is enough, she decided. Could she turn? Or must she back out?

Yes, back out.

She pushed with her left hand, felt pointed impact on her head, found herself sprawled in the water.

Ow!

Her eyes stung. She blinked away tears. *I'm big! I'm brave!*

She pulled her legs under her, kneeling, waiting for the sparkles that confused her vision to fade.

They didn't.

Silver scintillas turned bronze, turned gold. Something ahead glittered and shed light.

She crouched lower, creeping forward to see more. What was this strangeness?

There, where the water grew abruptly deeper, a marvel gleamed below the surface, embedded in the wall of the well shaft: a mosaic of turquoise and bronze and the green of old, old copper depicting a broad-bladed sword with an almost rectangular shape to its blade.

She stared, captivated by its beauty, wondering how such artistry came to be buried in the water. The light revealing the sword brightened, and she saw it wasn't truly a mosaic, but an actual weapon.

She stretched forward, reaching to touch it, maybe to grip its hilt.

Rust appeared on the edges of the blade, dark and crusted brown, flushing swiftly to scarlet, then dimming to wine red. Its glow blackened, illuminating her fingers strangely. Her hands seemed to curve, twisting her fingers into curling claws that dripped blood.

Remeya screamed.

"No!" she cried and scrabbled backward, turning the moment the tunnel permitted it, floundering wildly through the pools edging the stream and out into daylight.

Max scooped her out of the spring, guilt writ large on his boy's face, frantic hands gentled by his affection for her. "What happened? What happened?" he gasped.

She never told him.

If only I'd never told anyone. She shivered again, craving warmth, struggling to leave her memories behind, to regain today and the tourney.

If only Bernessa hadn't boasted about the magical tanager, an artifact her family sequestered in their home, the Castel Ghiquesa. If only Remeya hadn't revisited her little girl wish to be bigger and better than her friend. If only Remeya had not been impulsively moved to her own spurt of boasting about her adventure of the well.

But I did. I did.

And disaster loomed because of her. All because of her.

Remeya's gaze locked onto the scabbard at the king's belt: metal with the patina of copper verdigris, set with onyx, traced by bronze filigree. Beautiful, were it not for the miasma of dread exuding from the weapon within.

The trumpets blared again as a chestnut stallion—shining gold in the sunlight—entered the field.

This knight wore silver armor chased with gold. He was Lord Rollo, nephew and heir to Sevran— king of neighboring Eirdry—and beloved by him.

The clash between the dark knight and the bright should have been thrilling: the power of their striding mounts, lances shattering against shields, the athletic leap of the riders from their saddles, the flash of blades drawn from scabbards.

It *was* thrilling to the crowd in the stands, to the armsmen and lords before the pavilions, to the ladies in the royal box.

Remeya bit her lip, forced her hands away from her face, back to her sides.

What do I fear?

She hardly knew, but this was wrong, horribly wrong. She glanced upward at the lady next to her.

How had she come to stand again at the princess' elbow? Aeliana's face looked as strained as Remeya's felt. "Trust in our god, child," the princess murmured.

She senses it too. But what is it?

Remeya swallowed. "How might our Wild Lord intervene . . . in this?" she whispered.

"You must trust more than mere circumstances to him, Remeya. Trust *yourself* to him."

Remeya wasn't sure what that meant, and the action on the jousting ground scattered her attention.

Both combatants had doffed their great helms, trusting the cervellieres—steel skullcaps—worn underneath.

King Xavo's falchion showed a ribbon of blood. Was Lord Rollo injured?

He'd dropped his shield, but wielded his bastard sword with conviction, catching the falchion on its crossguard, jabbing the weak points of Xavo's armor with its point. His wound, if he had one, never slowed him.

Yet the king's blows were heavy, propelled by the weight of his falchion's massive blade.

Aeliana gasped. Remeya glanced up again. Aeliana's eyes were wide. Her trembling fingers touched her mouth. Remeya looked back to the joust as the crowd groaned.

Lord Rollo was down, sprawled in the dust, blood leaking from his lips.

"Dost thou yield?" bellowed Xavo.

Blessed Cathal! Did he not see that his foe could not answer?

"Yield, I adjure thee!"

Merciful Eoin! He did *not* see.

"Must I call thee dastard?" He brandished his falchion at the fallen knight's throat.

Remeya flinched.

Then the cirurgiens were there, clustering around Lord Rollo, restraining the lords who had surged onto the field to pacify the king.

"Your Majesty, he is fallen."

"Your Majesty, he lacks voice."

"Your Majesty, let us minister to him."

The king's face darkened. "He cowers whilst thou make his excuses!"

Princess Aeliana touched Remeya's shoulder. "Bide. Keep my ladies with you."

She hurried to the box stairs, flowed down the steep flight in a smooth rush, and came to her brother's side.

Remeya found herself unable to stem the maids and matrons in their own rush for the exit and followed the princess perforce, borne on the tide of women. She arrived at her patroness' elbow just as Aeliana curtsied and spoke.

"Your Majesty, victory crowns thee. Wilt thou not take refreshment before the melee?"

His reddened falchion was not yet sheathed.

Remeya held her breath. *Would he . . . ?*

The king whirled, narrowly missed petite Lady Varice with his blade, and strode for his pavilion.

The gathered lords accompanied their ruler, the cirurgiens renewed their attentions to Lord Rollo, and Aeliana knelt to add her prayers to their efforts.

"Horned Eoin, may your sacrifice make his unnecessary. May your spilt blood restore his. May your hunt chase his death from the world this time."

Remeya's own knees gave way, but she was not praying, not yet.

This time had been too like the other last year: King Xavo wroth, the falchion's blade bare, and witnesses clustered close.

If only I'd said that I could not. That I was faint. That the treasure—the sword—was gone from the water.

Could one say no to a king?

But he'd been so different when he asked her a year ago; before ever she'd fetched the falchion from its watery grave.

✝

A year ago he'd played Blind Man's Bluff with the fosterlings, volunteering as the blind man. He'd read to them in the evenings. And overruled the stablemaster who insisted that girls must use sidesaddles. He'd been . . . kind. Safe. Trustworthy.

When the story of her young exploit in the spring-tunnel passed from Bernessa to Linea to Lady Corenna to the princess and—at last—to the king, Remeya had blushed, but gotten over her embarrassment.

When he knelt before her and begged the boon of her courage and chivalry, she'd left both fear and regret for her lack of discretion behind in her wish to please him.

When she placed the falchion in his hands—herself wet and muddy and shaken a second time—and saw him draw the weapon, she knew she'd made a very great mistake.

She'd emerged from the tunnel, carefully not looking at her own aching hands holding the tongs clamped upon falchion's hilt.

The king's face held only encouragement, approval, and hope.

"Well done, child," he told her. "I stand in thy debt."

Then his hand circled the grip.

She'd never seen fear in his eyes before. Not when he faced down the wild aurochs charging Lady Juneya. Not when he scooped young Tito to safety from the top of his plunge off the battlements. Not even when Romulo surprised a bitter scorpion in his riding boots. Action married to cool aplomb, that was all he displayed.

When the falchion met his full grasp, fear passed through terror to something else on his face, another expression unknown to Remeya's experience of her sovereign. Could it be . . . horror? Surely not.

Then, with blade free of its scabbard, rage took him.

The lords and their armsmen scattered as the king cut the air in brutal strokes.

Trying the weapon's balance?

Xavo's hound—his favorite bitch, mother to the royal hunting pack and old in her devotion—wasn't fast enough.

It was terrifying to witness: faithful Matroniya whimpering as her blood soaked the dust while her master hacked the air and ignored her pain. Lord Pellucon dispatched the hound from her misery after Xavo whirled toward the bastion and strode away.

Remeya shuddered.

She wouldn't think of it. Not an instant past the moment in the well shaft when her own fingers faltered near the falchion's grip, protected by the tongs she'd brought with her. When pain bloomed deep in her joints. When worse . . . had not happened to *her*, but claimed her king instead. *It didn't happen,* she couldn't say. *None of it.*

Because it had.

If only she'd dropped the blade down into the darkness below the deepest water in the well. Down, far down, where none could fetch it up to the light of the sky. Or would the king merely have urged her to forsake air, lungs bursting, in a dive toward madness.

The frantic voices of the cirurgiens recalled Remeya to the present.

"Your Highness, no! His blood is tainted. Do not!"

Princess Aeliana bent to give the kiss of life, blowing the breath of her breast through the slack lips of the fallen.

Lady Corenna's words were calmer. "Princess, Lord Rollo is dead."

Aeliana raised her head.

"This fault is mine." Guilt haunted her eyes. "Had I but swallowed my words, Lord Rollo would live."

Remeya started. *But it is my doing, my boasting, my journey under the earth. How could it be hers? She'd been the last in the chain of rumor, not the first. I started it.*

"Our sovereign wielded the blade that slew, not thee, Princess."

If Princess Aeliana were innocent, was Remeya?

I don't care if I'm innocent or not. I just wish this had never happened.

The cirurgiens summoned the churls with their litter. Aeliana's ladies were urging the princess to her bower. Bernessa clutched Remeya's hands, weeping. There could be no recalling of words or deeds or events. Only the preparations for Lord Rollo's funeral rites remained.

✝

Princess Aeliana and her ladies retired. The tournament's royal box went empty. Behind them, Xavo ordered the melee—the final contest of the festival, in which all those entered in the lists fought together against one another—to proceed.

Leaving the tourney in the princess' wake, Remeya considered her homecoming two weeks prior— her third during the two years that had passed since she left to join Aeliana's retinue.

She'd grown closer to her father after she'd departed. That seemed so strange. Surely their hearts should cool when months passed between their meetings.

But they'd exchanged letters often. He seemed to forget she was a child and included long accounts of the challenges he faced running Castel Baloron and managing its people. Maybe that's why she liked him better. In ink on parchment, he respected her. Was less critical. Forbore to scold her whenever her behavior didn't fit his idea of a lady's demeanor.

Well, he couldn't scold. He wasn't there in Castel Cincrestes to *see* her race Bernessa in the Long Gallery. Or the time she and one of the pageboys hid a hedgehog quill under the seat cushion of the sententious Master of the King's Music. Or how she always rode astride, not sidesaddle, now.

And the princess and the king just laughed at her antics. Or they had.

Her father had missed her so much, that first six months, he'd begged Aeliana for a visit from his daughter while the princess guested with her uncle in Eirdry, the neighboring kingdom.

Remeya's father had embraced his daughter tenderly upon her return. Arranged that the evening's supper should feature all her favorite dishes—figgy fish paté and lemon sherbet. And played his mandolin for her at retiring time.

She'd slept in her own bedchamber during that first visit home.

Upon her second return to Baloron, she'd arrived as one of Aeliana's retinue, and bided in the princess' chambers. That had been the disastrous sojourn when she retrieved the falchion for the king. Remeya bit her lip.

Now, during this third homecoming, she'd traveled again amongst Aeliana's household. And slumbered not in her own bedchamber, but in an apartment adjacent to the royal suites, remaining within call of her mistress. But after she'd seen the princess settled that first afternoon, she'd sought her old room. Not to re-visit old times and familiar places, no.

To re-connect with her old nurse.

And Nerilla was there, just as her assistant in the castle stillroom said she would be.

Remeya had paused on the stone threshold of her bedchamber, taking everything in. The tall, dark bed, canopied in forest green brocade, had scared her the first night she'd ever slept in it, a nursery baby newly removed from the nursery. Now, it looked . . . cozy, but somehow too small. Was her sleeping couch at Castel Cincrestes so much bigger? No. No, it was not. But she'd changed, since she last dreamt in this room.

The wall tapestries embroidered with scenes of a lady's garden remained as colorful and cheerful as she remembered, a riot of pink and yellow and apricot. Nurse had dredged them up from some forgotten store when baby Remeya's screaming nightmares continued each night after that first awful one. It had worked, too. Small Remeya had slept sound thereafter.

Now, the strong autumn sun shone through the small, cloudy panes of the generous window behind the cushioned window seat. A bright square of light glowed on the patterned maroon carpeting.

As Remeya watched, Nerilla rummaged in one of the curiously carved teak chests along the walls. A uncut bolster of cream silk, a pair of gilt sandals, and a spinning top tumbled out onto the carpeted floor. Nerilla uttered a muffled exclamation and straightened with some smaller item clutched in her hand. She pursed her lips. Did she hear something? She turned toward the doorway, and her plump, wrinkled face—framed by its pale wimple and dark cowl—beamed.

"Lovey!"

Remeya ran into Nerilla's arms. Oh! the comfort of those soft arms and dumpy body! And the sweet smell of the rose petal potpourri Nerilla strewed in her clothes chest to keep the moth at bay! Its scent enfolded Remeya, taking her straight back to those nursery days, when she was safe, and Nurse knew all the answers.

Nerilla drew back from the embrace, studied Remeya's face—she had to look up to do it—patted Remeya's cheek, and clucked. "Dear, dear, it will be alright."

"Will it?" Remeya's voice sounded tremulous in her own ears. If only Nurse *did* have all the answers.

"Have you supped?" asked Nerilla. "Worry feeds on hunger, lovey."

Remeya nodded. "Aeliana insisted." So wise for her retinue, so neglectful of herself. The fish broth had tasted delicious, savory and salty, delicate in its flavor. But Aeliana took none.

They'd all known something was far awry the instant they'd ridden under Castel Baloron's gatehouse, there to dismount.

Remeya's father had awaited them, pale and trembling. He'd exerted himself to greet the princess properly, bending in the deep, sweeping bow accorded to royalty, and uttering sonorous words of welcome. He'd ordered the stable boys to tend their horses. He'd guided the princess to her chambers, sparing a worried smile for his daughter.

His facade of court etiquette unnerved Remeya more than if he'd owned how shaken he felt. She'd seen Papere shaken, especially in the years after her mother's death. But shaken and pretending not to be? Never.

King Xavo had arrived before them by some turns of the glass. As they'd passed by the doors to his chambers, they'd heard raised voices. The page boys who brought the fish broth had refused to meet their eyes.

"Nerilla, what happened? Surely the king has not decided to give Baloron to the Order of Adrealle?"

That possibility, when raised at court half a year before, had seemed so far-fetched that Remeya had laughed. Indeed, Xavo himself refused to take it seriously, leaning toward the gift of a different castle to the monks. And yet . . .

Her nurse drew Remeya close for a sideways squeeze, her soft heavy arm around Remeya's waist, then urged her toward the window seat.

The sun felt warm on her back, a welcome heat, since no brazier warmed the cool stone of her bedchamber. A small puff of dust escaped from the dark green bolster as she and Nerilla settled on the bench. Remeya stifled a sneeze.

Nerilla's expression clouded.

"Little Bennis—my assistant's son—grew so frightened when his majesty's stallion entered the gatehouse."

Remeya could imagine it. The massive black steed loomed like a mountain, the gleam of rage in his eyes. She'd be scared, too, were she afoot and Morke advancing on her.

"Bennis made the sign of our Horned Lord." Ah, the spread forefinger and middle finger, palm toward the signer. "And the king saw him."

Remeya felt her chest go tense and cold. "And the little one? Small Bennis?"

"Unharmed," Nerilla reassured her. "But the king is wroth, blaming Baloron's elders for the infant's poor morals and speculating on the cleansing effect the monks might have on the castle community."

Remeya's breath came sharply. "He *is* giving Baloron to the monks?"

Nerilla's mouth eased. "No. Not yet. But . . . 'tis no auspicious beginning."

No. Indeed, no. And the king . . . one could not trust him as he was now.

She'd wondered if he had contracted the troll-disease. Trolls were human—sane—before they sickened. Then the illness stole their humanity, and with it their compassion. Their ability to walk in another's sandals vanished. Worse, they grew malicious. Like King Xavo.

So, she'd wondered.

But trolls suffered physical deformities long before insanity eroded their wits.

King Xavo remained as comely as ever: black-haired, black-bearded, strong and straight of limb. No hint of the hunched back, the sagging skin, or the elongated nose typical of a troll.

Besides, she knew when his savagery began: the instant he gripped the lost falchion.

No, Xavo's madness was something altogether other than troll-disease.

Remeya gazed longingly at her old nurse's wrinkled face. Nerilla seemed just as steady and certain as she always had. How did she stay so serene amidst ill happenings? Remeya wanted her secret.

Nerilla held a diminutive mahogany box in her age-twisted fingers. Was that what she'd removed from the chest? Carved leaves and a tracery of vines adorned its small sides. Nerilla lifted its shallow lid. Inside glinted the shimmer of gold. She drew a fine chain from it. As the chain came free of its container, the pendant on the delicate links swung forward. It was a stag, the antlers angled back over its head and neck to form a loop through which the chain might pass.

"Oh!" Remeya's own hand spasmed in the sign of the Horned One.

"We didn't know Aeliana was one of us, when you were invited to her service. How risky it'd be to store a Gedier symbol amongst your jewels. But now . . ."

But now . . . they knew the princess worshipped at Cummenos' altar. Even though her brother eschewed the old religion and cleaved to the disciplines of *pensare*— meditation, postural sequences, and enlightenment. Did she revere Cummenos in defiance of the king? Remeya had not thought it, but now it seemed so.

"Surely 'tis riskier now than ever to flaunt such a thing!" But, oh, she wanted her pendant and the comfort of her Divine Father's own signifier.

"Flaunt it?" chided Nerilla. "No. But tuck it hidden beneath your chemise, or hidden in your casket whilst you bathe? Yes."

Yes. Oh, yes, indeed.

Remeya remembered debating the bestowal of the pendant when she left home. To leave it? To take it?

Which was best? Which safest? To risk her immortal soul? Or to risk her exposure at court?

Then her father took a hand in the issue.

✝

She'd bade him farewell in Baloron's solar. Two years ago in autumn.

The strong seasonal sun bathed the room in light, shining through the less cloudy—and more costly—panes of the grouped windows, golden and warm. The bright scarlet and aqua of the cushions and hangings glowed, almost like Remeya's casket of jewels. And the satin smooth mahogany of the chairs and tables and chests shone like the feathers of the red-breasted hawk.

She'd wondered if her father would bother to wish her safe journey, but he'd sent for her when the churls came for the last of her trunks.

Standing before him in the solar, she'd stared up at his face. Just a little up. He wasn't a big man—sturdy and square, yes, but not tall—and she'd grown in the last few months.

His mouth held its usual uncompromising line, as though he would never lose anything precious ever again, if he just refused to smile. But his eyes . . . something was different about his eyes. Were their hazel depths softer?

He straightened and shifted his stance wider. The amber brocade of his robe hushed across his boot tops.

"I've tolerated your flirtation with the old religion," he began abruptly. "I know it brought you comfort after your mother's death. Made it easier to get on with your nurse."

Flirtation? She bit back a hot defense of her devotion to the Horned One. But, flirtation? Is that what he called years of prayer and ritual and worship?

"But it's frowned upon by the pontiff, feared by the peasantry, despised at court."

"Despised?" Her lips formed the words, soundless. She knew the king practiced the modern *pensare* discipline. She'd thought his preference mild and politic, not passionate. But, despised? Surely the old religion was merely a little embarrassing. Like her cuddling a dolly at bedtime or Nurse fingering her rosary beads.

"I'll be discrete," she reassured her father.

"No. I should have spoken to you before now, but discretion isn't enough. You must forego all outward demonstration of your faith. No spoken prayer. No ritual gestures. No attending the secret rites. If there are any in Castel Cincrestes."

Dismay held her silent a moment.

"But, Father! My belief is not an amusement!" She heard her voice going high and child-like.

"Perhaps not. But that is my decree."

She'd obeyed, pulling the stag pendant out of her jewel casket and pressing it upon Nerilla. Stilling her hands when her fingers moved to make the sign of the Horned One. Never touching her brow in homage to his Holy Hermit.

Until she'd discovered the princess followed the old beliefs. Discretely, in private, but not invisibly or without outward manifestation.

They'd prayed together at Aeliana's portable shrine. Attended the equinox vigil together. And now she was to wear her beloved pendant again.

Nerilla fastened the clasp behind her neck. The weight of the stag felt anchoring against her breast. She tucked it beneath her chemise, the gold warm on her skin, warmed by Nerilla's fingers.

She'd found her hand drawn to its heartening weight again and again in the fortnight since her nurse had restored it to her. Now, as she trailed in the wake of the princess' retinue, trying not to see Lord Rollo's slack body in her mind's eye, she touched the lump the pendant made under her gown, the sharpness of its antlers pricking her thumb.

The Holy Hermit Cathal had single-handedly bent the Gedier faith toward inward contemplation and symbolic sacrifice rather than death sacrifice. But five hundred years after Cathal's martyrdom, the heretic Bellam had preached a return to the old ways of blood and violence. He'd declared the Gedier faith vitiated and in need of revitalization. He'd done more than speak; for a decade he'd presided over a sect that ritually slayed a sacral king each year at the harvest. With the result that the old religion—faltering in truth—was declared anathema.

But for Bellam, Remeya could wear her stag pendant openly.

The dry, tan grasses of the outer bailey—due for a scything—rustled unpleasantly against Remeya's skirt. She swallowed, her throat hot and tight, and looked up at the sky, so high and blue and clear; an autumn sky, when the air felt cool, but the sun's rays, warm.

The muttering growl of the tourney crowd—awaiting the start of the melee—faded behind her. The softer murmur of the ladies faded ahead of her slow pace. They would pass through the gatehouse to the inner bailey considerably before her. Remeya's eyes clung to the soft red of Baloron's walls. Her home. Her shelter. They brought no comfort now.

The brief, wild cry of a hawk pierced the gentle breeze.

A vision of Lord Rollo boiled into her awareness, his face pale and vacant under his warrior's skullcap, eyes fixed and flat, lips leaking blood. His armor-cased body flung down in the dust, empty of his animating spirit.

Remeya's hot, tight throat grew hotter and tighter. The residue of sweetened wine she'd sipped after Max's bout cloyed in her mouth. She longed for cold, chill spring water—anything—to relieve the torrid weight of death on her soul.

For a moment, she envisioned the king's falchion when she retrieved it, cool turquoise and jade glimmering under limpid liquid. The start of all this dread.

Then her thoughts took her further back in time to her first exploration under the earthen arch, wading through its buried stream. Her mother had sickened only weeks before, coughing up blood and weary, unable to leave her bed. She'd died so slowly and yet so fast, lingering on for months of suffering, then gone, utterly gone, forever.

The teachers of the *pensare* had insisted Remeya view her mother's body.

"She must know the Lady Irsiva to be dead, not merely absent, which would be harmful."

And, oh, she knew.

In the dim chamber, strong sunlight had cast the shadows into deeper gloom. Dust motes gleamed in the flood of brilliance streaming through the clouded glass of the eastern window.

Remeya had fought them at the doorway, pulling against their strong arms, kicking. They dragged her within, into the stale sickroom smell, right up to the curtained bed with its rumpled sheets and quilts, its mound of cushions. And Mamere.

They'd not even washed Mamere's body or made all tidy for the funeral rites.

Her dark curling tresses spread out across the pillow. Her white nightgown was stained with old sweat. Her limbs lay tumbled like the bedclothes. Had her last agonies been so troubled?

Face pale and vacant, like Lord Rollo's.

Oh, Remeya knew her mother was dead.

Then she'd screamed. Now she walked into the shadow of Baloron's gatehouse and fled across the paved courtyard of the inmost bailey, her scurrying form small beneath the looming curtain walls and the massive central keep. She dove for the narrow sally port in the passage between the portcullis and the great hall, seeking the dark and twisting spiral up, more private than the grand stairway further in.

The cold stone steps hurt her feet through the thin soles of her slippers.

Up and up and up.

She felt a sob crowd her throat.

Then she was there, approaching refuge, in front of the polished mahogany door to her guest chamber near the princess' suite. The bronze latch gave under her trembling hand, admitting her to light and warmth.

So different from her chamber in her father's quarters, bright not dark, this apartment featured furnishings of blond northern woods, cushions in butter yellow silk, sun shining through the rare clear glass of its window panes.

The ache in her throat ebbed as she sat on one of two backless chairs and kicked off her slippers. The bolster under her thighs felt solid and comforting. She wriggled her stockinged feet in the patch of sun on the amber carpeting.

As fast as the memories and emotions had seized her, they faded.

Those stupid *pensareans*! If Nurse had known what they intended, she'd have stopped them. She did stop them when they prescribed extra devotions for the ease of Remeya's spirit: the dawn posture sequence upon rising; joy mudras—finger movements—before luncheon; and the dusk postures before sleeping. Ugh! Plus a healthy helping of chanting.

Nerilla had said no. Or, no! And made it stick. "The little thing's naught but six years of age, and that's too much."

Instead she'd taken Remeya to a private Gedier service in the old chapel. Voices and footfalls murmured in the vaulted space. Colors glowed, light passing through the red and blue and green and purple stained glass windows.

She'd not understood the ritual, but the calls of the priestess followed by the responses of the worshippers— back and forth—had soothed the young Remeya. The bread broken before it was buried tasted fresh and wholesome. The cool water with which they'd washed her feet eased the hot ache in her chest.

Every man and woman in that small gathering—had it been a dozen?—touched her head or her wrist and spoke a blessing for her.

Not knowing the risks, not understanding anything about the old beliefs, she'd converted on the spot.

Despite the scary scene in the window above the wooden bench on which she'd sat. It depicted the Holy Hermit in the sacrifice by which Cummenos was drawn down from heaven into his earthly manifestation, there to hunt dark evil into hell.

The hermit hung head down, dangling from a rope tied around his ankles and slung over the bough of a great oak. He stretched out his arms while blood poured from the wound in his chest. Love transfigured his face.

The Holy Hermit—Cathal—had lived and died one thousand two hundred years ago, but the Gedier still honored his gift in their rites. The old believers, before Bellam's heresy, had re-enacted it with a lamb in Cathal's place. The newer ones, following Bellam's defeat, merely re-lived Cathal's sacrifice in the symbols of wine and bread and in story.

Remeya had never regretted her conversion. Neither when she'd learned more about her faith, nor as the beliefs grew steadily more condemned by the monarchy and the court.

The old religion had enjoyed a few revivals in the centuries since its banning, but the current one had been brief indeed. The chapel windows were boarded over now, and the Gedier rites performed only before personal shrines or secretly in the countryside.

Remeya pulled the stag pendant out from under her chemise. The curve of its antlers, the smooth shine of the gold, and the warmth of the metal from its close contact with her breast calmed her. Reluctantly, she tucked it away again, slid her slippers back on her feet, and rose.

The princess would miss her, if Remeya stayed sulking in her chamber over long. Her station as fosterling and maid-in-waiting meant she must attend at Aeliana's pleasure, not her own.

✝

The shadowed corridor outside her room felt unwelcomingly cool as she walked along it. Glad to quit its chill, set her hand to the heavy door of the princess' apartments, pushed it open, and entered the warmth of the small anteroom with the glow of the royal solar beyond. Brocades in apricot and gold against mahogany couches kindled the generous, curving space. But it didn't feel lively, for all the bright color and restless movement within it. It should have, but it didn't.

Surrounding Aeliana, her ladies twittered and fluttered, still reacting to Lord Rollo's death. Remeya heard murmurs—"he's a troll, he's a troll" and "no, he isn't, he can't be"—as she threaded her way through them. King Xavo *acted* like a troll from the old legends, but truly his insanity was too sudden for that to be true. Remeya brushed against one of the many standing screens dividing the room. It wobbled, but did not fall.

The princess sat in a backless chair leaning her shoulders against a floral tapestry on the wall behind her. Her gaze rested on the floor. Her hands lay in her lap. She looked defeated.

Remeya knelt before her mistress.

"Your Highness, shall I summon the lute player to solace the hour?"

Aeliana looked up. Her face lightened slightly.

"There's a promising thought, child. Do."

The mellow notes of the instrument hushed the fidgeting ladies and eased the princess' strain. Remeya herself sang at Aeliana's request, a lullaby for a baby's slumber and then an old Gedier hymn, still popular at court despite its taboo origins.

Tall Lady Juneya drew the traveling set of Towers and Riders from a low cabinet, setting the checkered board of maple and ebony on a table, and placing the agate pieces in the starting arrangement. Aeliana chose the red side and pressed the crystal—with its opening move—on Remeya. Somberly, they played as the afternoon passed toward evening.

When the light slanted low through the western windows, page boys lit the oil lamps. The sun slid behind a bank of cloud lying on the horizon, and the lamps shone in the sudden dusk. Word came that no knights had perished in the melee nor suffered grievous wounds.

Remeya let go a breath she'd not known she was holding.

The king's squire, young Lord Ezek, arrived to escort the princess to the banquet at day's end.

She refused.

Remeya felt her chest tightening, in-breaths growing shallow again.

When King Xavo appeared in the archway between the solar and its antechamber, she knew why.

He'd bathed and changed his garb. The resplendence of his amber and russet striped doublet and round hose, his cream velvet cape, declared his pleasure in his prowess at the tourney, but a sense of impending violence emanated from him.

Gaze stern and chin firm, he waited, poised to chide his sister.

She rose from her seat and curtsied.

"Dismiss thy ladies."

"As thy Majesty wills it." She gestured. The Ladies Juneya and Varice mustered the others toward the antechamber. They averted their eyes as they passed close by their sovereign. Remeya, last in the straggling line, delayed at the archway.

The king stepped forward.

Remeya slid behind the tapestry against which Aeliana had leaned all afternoon, moving into a niche in the thick stone wall. Peering around the edge of the woolen hanging, she saw Xavo and Aeliana confront one another, yet standing.

Despite his disapproval, the king's voice was mild,

albeit formal. "Thou wouldst scorn thy guests? 'Tis the lady's courtesy to preside over her board." Indeed, the princess had never forsaken such feasts in the past.

Aeliana gazed at him, saying nothing. Her eyes were cold.

"My lords must sup."

Still nothing from his sister.

"I shall don umbrous mourning and require my lords to do likewise." Was the king pleading? Remeya bit her lip. Hard. It hurt, and the salt of blood flooded her mouth.

Her brother's plea pierced the princess' chill reserve. Aeliana knelt suddenly, covering her face with her hands.

The king's brow darkened. Would he strike her?

Then his eyes softened. "Dear heart, forgive me." He bent to raise her, encircling her shoulders in gentle embrace. His words paralleled this tender intimacy. "All shall be ordered as you wish. Instruct me."

"Grief is my feast," choked Aeliana, and she clung to him. He held her, his face echoing her sorrow. So. Despite their differences, this royal brother and sister still loved one another. *Like my father and me.* Except...not like. Papere adhered to the proper and royally sanctioned *pensare* disciplines, yes. But he tolerated the old beliefs with some appreciation for their benefits. Unlike the king, who tolerated the Gedier faith primarily by ignoring it.

Remeya gnawed one knuckle. Would Aeliana's faith, could it, prove Xavo's redemption? He looked so sad. Almost she crept to his side, forsaking her shelter. No. She didn't belong here. Her comfort would be intrusion only. His sister's must suffice. And if it did not?

Remeya stood still.

Xavo released Aeliana to her backless chair, steadying her a moment, restoring her arms to the armrests. "Tell me," he urged.

Remeya edged to one side of her niche, trying to keep both king and princess in sight.

"I would have Lord Rollo's last rite conducted in the manner of the Gedier," answered Xavo's sister. "He professed the cervine faith."

Cathal Revered! Why profess her own taboo faith now, of all times? The king knew of her leanings, yes, but now was no moment in which to remind him of them! Remeya shrank against the tower wall, its stones chill through the thin silk of her gown and the equally thin lawn of her chemise. *She must not! Must not!*

Xavo drew back. "The Creed of the Horned One was never reinstated!" *Indeed, it remained forbidden.*

"Many profess it nonetheless." Aeliana raised her chin.

Xavo's brow darkened. "The royal house must not be amongst their number!"

"The royal house might be first amongst their number."

"Blood and violence birthed the Gedier. Blood and violence shadowed all their long history. And blood and violence brought them down. Their reinstatement would be an evil act." *It was true.* Ritual sacrifice—human sacrifice—had featured in the ceremonies of the Gedier from their very beginnings more than three thousand years ago. The creed was birthed by primitive tribes, desperate to control the fertility of the soil, and then continued by more civilized folk. Although the city-states of two thousand years ago reserved the blood rite for times of extremity only—drought and famine, pestilence, or defense against a mighty enemy.

But the believers in Cathal's time had grown degenerate. Criminals and cripples were anointed and slain under the guise of devotion, with entertainment as the true purpose. *But not now. Never now.* The Holy Hermit had changed all that. Remeya's throat felt cold and tight.

Aeliana's chin firmed. She looked down. Did the princess perceive more violence in her brother than in the old religion? Remeya shivered.

"I spoke my vows on Cummenos' Eve this winter last."

Xavo whitened.

"You didn't!" he whispered.

"The renewed *deor*-faith is different," insisted Aeliana. "Cathal's tale of self-sacrifice and redemption holds our hearts. Bellam's votary of power and death, not at all; 'tis considered heresy."

Xavo's mouth tightened. "The roots of the Gedier beliefs won't vanish for your entreaty, dear sister. They are there. They are strong. They but wait for opportunity. Forsake your vows, I beg you."

"Never." Some of the king's steel rang in her voice.

Remeya touched the tapestry that hid her. The wool smelled faintly of lanolin—sheep oil—faintly of cinnamon, the potpourri favored by Aeliana. Was Xavo an outward manifestation of ferocity, Aeliana an inward one?

"To please me?" said the king.

Aeliana's nostrils pinched, and her lips straightened. *Not the right plea.*

Xavo's temporary tenderness transformed into coercion. "I forbid you to profess your faith!" Courtly language—thou and thy—left behind in intimacy, remained absent in his anger.

"You are too late!" She gave him back defiance for his constraint. "I have forsaken my birth name. I am now Aoife!"

The king's eyes blazed. "I declare you in contempt of

your sovereign's will." He swallowed, reclaimed courtly diction. "Thou art treasonous!"

The princess stood, gathering formality herself. "Dost thou declare the Eirdrean tradition of beheading sororal claimants to the throne less violent than Bellam's transformations of shadow into light?" she flung at him. *That was true, too.* The kings of Eirdry—the neighboring realm—had once slain their sisters to keep the lines of descent unconfused.

Xavo's fingers touched the pommel of his falchion, a black opal entire, with the shadow of some green stone behind it. Remeya held her breath. Then the king's hand fell to his side, and he turned, but did not storm away.

Remeya breathed again.

Xavo stood silent a time, then spoke, his back still turned. "Sister, there is reason and quietude in the contemplation of balance. Our Istrian *pensare*—pursuit of serenity, courage, and wisdom—stems only from love. Canst thou not embrace it once more? The perils of a personal deity—tribalism, zealousness, fanaticism—are real." Was that anguish in his voice?

More truth. The approved religion of Istria worshipped no deity, but pursued disciplines of meditation.

The princess reseated herself. "My courage and hope never burgeoned so strong from mere meditation. Love of the Horned One hath made me brave; contemplation of balance dost not infuse my timidity with valor. I shall not forswear myself." *No, she would not.*

Xavo turned around. "So be it."

"Lord Rollo?"

"Shall receive rites of transformation and passage in the traditions of wisdom." The *pensare.*

"And myself?"

Now the king did stride away. Pausing in the antechamber, he declared over one shoulder, "*Aoife* . . . thou shalt go to the tower and the blade."

Aoife lifted her chin.

The king passed out of her chambers, his tread swift on the stairs.

✝

Remeya felt as cold as the stone at her back. *Blessed Cathal!* Could this be real? Aeliana declared treasonous? Sentenced to death?

Remeya wanted to rush to Aeliana's side, but something stopped her. The tilt of the royal head, the chill in her eyes. She was dangerous, and certainly no source of comfort or reassurance. Even had she been of a mood to offer the encouragement Remeya wanted, what consolation was there? The princess' own brother had condemned her. Remeya couldn't quite believe it. Had the king truly said those words, "Thou shalt go to the tower and the blade"? And, having said them, would he not repent of them?

Remeya's sense of unreality fled only when Lord Ezek and Lord Merral came for the princess.

They took her to Tower Nuvolat, the tallest on the curtain wall of the outer bailey, and locked her in the Queen's Bower. Aeliana—*Aoife*, Remeya reminded herself—was no queen, merely sister to the king, but the bower was the customary repository for any royal prisoner. It had acquired its name when Xavo's great grandfather locked his consort away there for life. She'd conspired with his enemies to take the Istrian throne for herself.

Remeya visited Aoife, bringing sweetmeats from the hands of her ladies and restraining her own tears. *Crying won't help her,* Remeya told herself fiercely. *She needs help, not weeping.*

Four weeks passed. But Remeya couldn't think of any help—real help—she could bring. Aoife told her to pray, but how would mere petition achieve anything? Aoife needed deeds, not words.

Then Remeya did think of something.

She persuaded Bernessa to ride out with her on a pleasure jaunt to the ruins of Ysbrydion Hill—the old stone circle that once held dark rituals to Cummenos—and convinced the stable grooms that *two* maids needed no escort.

Bernessa complained from the moment Remeya proposed the expedition. She complained all the way down to the stables and out through the gatehouse. "How can you think of pleasure and fun when the princess is sentenced to death? I don't feel like riding. I never liked it much anyway. Why the ruins? They're creepy and shivery." And so on.

Remeya waited until the Castel Baloron shrank to a dot on the hillside behind them and the dust of the dry grasslands rose beneath their mounts' hoofs before she confessed their true destination.

Bernessa liked that no better.

"Do you want to go to the Nuvol-tower yourself?" she protested. "The Gediers' High Holy Hind lives in seclusion for a reason. You'll get *her* tossed in prison along with both of us!"

Remeya sighed. "She won't boast of our visit. And we shouldn't. How will anyone know? The horses?"

Bernessa giggled. "There is that legend of the horse who was really a troll and could speak."

Remeya didn't snort, remembering all Aeliana's—no, *Aoife's*—lessons in ladylike behavior. And then she did snort. On horseback with one intimate friend wasn't court. Surely being ladylike needn't apply to all the hours between sunup and sundown.

Unfortunately Orloitha's advice dovetailed with that of the princess: pray!

Resisting the high priestess of the entire Gedier order felt disrespectful, but Remeya wanted something more than that to carry back to Tower Nuvolat.

"What do you think prayer is for?" asked Orloitha.

Remeya's lips parted. Then she stammered, "T-to sh-show obedience and faith?" The apostles of *pensare* would hate that guess. Did that mean it was right for the Gedier?

Orloitha was shaking her head. "Try it," she suggested. "You'll learn."

"But I want something that I know will work," insisted Remeya.

Orloitha's face turned sad. "Don't we all, child," she murmured, "don't we all."

Her maidservant pressed chilled grapes upon them as they reclined on the Hind's brocaded divans. Once the girls were rested, Orloitha gave them a message of encouragement for Aoife. And with that Remeya had to be content.

They rode home.

In Baloron's stable mews, Remeya watched Bernessa walk along the cobblestones between the wooden box stalls, trailing her horse and the churl leading him. Was Bernessa really going to curry her mount herself? Surely they should return to Aoife. They'd been away all afternoon.

Remeya wrinkled her nose and turned slowly toward the wide stable doors, open behind her. Maybe her friend had the right idea. Remeya felt equally reluctant to move on.

The late autumn sunshine—still strong here in the south—engoldened the sandstone paving and walls of the courtyard outside. The dim space of the stable, with its small square windows made smaller by partially closed shutters, felt almost cozy and safe, protected by its heavy wooden beams and its mundane function. No tense courtiers or angry kings loitered here.

She could hear the stable boys around an inner corner calling to one another, teasing while shoveling manure. A horse snorted in a nearby stall while another shifted, making that comfortable stirring sound that attends a large beast moving with ease.

Remeya leaned against a solid center pillar. Its rough, splintery surface pressed against her upper back, but couldn't scratch her through the layers of tabard, gown, and chemise. The thin silk of her hose and the sturdier linen of her split skirt clung to her inner thighs, sweat-dampened.

I should bathe.

She dug a hand into the pouch hanging from her belt, coming up with a last nugget of crystallized honey, gritty and sticky. Perhaps she'd follow Bernessa's example and tend to her mount. He'd appreciate the sweet morsel.

She inhaled. Dusty hay, oiled leather, warm horses.

The sound of brisk bootsteps and jingling spurs brought her head erect. She tensed.

A young man strode around an inner corner, a silhouette in the dimness. He was geared up for traveling: riding leathers strapped to his legs, his liege lord's device—black wolf against white and tan quarters—vaguely apparent on his tabard, and full saddlebags dangling from one strong hand.

The light from one unshuttered window flashed across his face, which proved a familiar one.

"Maximo!"

She felt her shoulders settling back down as she gazed at him, taking in the confident motion of him, the friendly look in his hazel eyes, the jaunty mustache—new—on his upper lip. He looked like someone who knew what to do about most things. But then, he always had. Maybe she didn't have to manage all alone.

"Max!" she called again.

He checked, squinting.

Right. She was likely just a shadow against the brilliance of the courtyard.

"Remeya?" Setting his saddlebags down on the cobblestones, he strode closer, his face relaxing when he got near. He took her hands.

"Remeya, what is it? What are you doing here?"

Abruptly her temporary calm deserted her. "Oh, Max! I went to see the High Holy Hind, but she doesn't know what to do either!"

His fingers pressed hers warningly. Leaving his saddlebags, he drew her into a nook beside the tack room and onto the stone bench beneath a shelf full of buckets. The bench felt cool through her damp skirt.

Max let go of her hands to place his palms on her shoulders.

"Remeya, what are you about?"

"I have to help the princess. I *have to*. I can't let her be . . . let her be . . ." A sob shook her before she could suppress it."

Max's friendly eyes flattened. "Remeya, this conflict is a royal matter, far over your head. You must let it be."

"Let Aoife be killed?! Oh, no!" Her voice rose.

"Ssh!" Max gave her shoulders a small shake.

"Max, every believer is called to be a saint," she hissed. "It is *not* above me to act."

Max's hands fell to his knees. "And you are a believer."

"You know I am."

"Remeya, the legends of the old heroes and martyrs are inspiring, but real life isn't like that. You needn't fling yourself into danger just to prove yourself devout and worthy. Self-preservation is a reasonable person's option too."

That gave her pause. Hadn't her own complaint about Aoife been just that? To show a little self-preservation. Except . . . perhaps Aoife hit some inner limit, beyond which a critical integrity was lost?

Remeya gripped the tops of Max's hands, there on his knees.

"The High Holy Hind told me to pray, but there has to be something we can actually *do*. Praying! Just praying is the same as doing nothing."

"The Hind told you that, did she?" Max's gaze grew suddenly intent.

Remeya nodded.

"Then you should do it."

"But you're not religious."

"No, I'm not an old believer."

"Then how can you recommend prayer? You don't even follow the disciplines of the *pensare*." She felt an unwelcome hollowness, disappointment rising in her chest. For a moment, when she'd first set eyes on him in that flash of light from a window, she'd been sure Max would have an answer. He'd seemed so competent, so certain. She couldn't believe he was echoing Orloitha.

"That's not really true," he chided. "I don't study the philosophy. Or believe it, either."

That shocked her, Gedier that she was. She'd grown up with the *pensare* and its doctrinal assertion that chanting, meditation, and postures ensured health of both mind and body. Even though the *pensare* had done nothing for her in the aftermath of her mother's death, surely it was . . . right. Good.

"But I perform the postural sequences daily," Max continued, "and I do find value in them. The priests— and your High Holy Hind—are not fools."

"But . . ."

"Remeya, I *must* go. Lord Graezon sends me to his stronghold to order the men-at-arms to prepare for war. For siege."

For war? She felt her lips shape the words soundlessly.

Scenes from the tourney—but a month ago—arose

from memory. The bright banners and the herald's horns. The shouts from the crowd. The crash of lance on shield. Her own excitement. Max claiming his guerdon.

The knightly bouts were real.

But war would not be like that.

War would be . . . like King Xavo cutting Lord Rollo down.

She searched Max's face. His eyes softened, his affection for her slowing his impetus toward his duty to his liege.

"Sevran of Eirdry will not leave his heir unavenged. My Lord Graezon knows this, even if our king has forgotten it."

She felt foolish. Like a child, she'd been thinking that one great trouble—the fate of the princess—held other troubles at bay. Now, war coming—she was sure Max (and Lord Graezon) was right—Aoife destined for death, *and* Baloron likely to pass out of her father's keeping. What next bad thing might arrive?

"Remeya." Max's voice, warm and steady, recalled her attention. "I don't meditate or pray, but this one thing I do know. The practice of a discipline often remains obscure in the doing of it. Later, its worth shows itself, but only if you've been faithful. I practice the *pensare* postures along with my knightly exercises. Do you pray!"

He was smiling. "You needn't believe me. Just do it."

She nodded convulsively.

He raised her hand to his lips, warm and firm against her skin.

Then he was up and moving, scooping his saddlebags from the cobblestones and striding away on his lord's commission.

So she prayed.

A lot.

Upon waking, before breaking her fast, at the close of noontide dinner, before she supped, and bending beside her bedtime couch.

Sometimes she felt holy, once exalted, often despairing, and most times: nothing at all.

How could this help? How could Orloitha be content to recommend nothing else? Was she really just praying there alone in her priory? Or did she organize a daring escape?

Bernessa took to avoiding her friend as the Ladies Varice and Corenna looked askance at Remeya's sudden access of religious devotion. The Istrian practice of *pensare* encouraged inward observance over outward gesture. Excessive prayer was a bad sign, not a good one. And Gedier prayer was even worse.

✝

One day during the prolonged waiting of Aoife's incarceration, tall Lady Juneya suggested they repair to the long gallery that connected the keep to the armory block, there to view the heroes of old, rendered in sculpted marble.

"We need their courage, their example, now more than ever," she declared. "Perhaps their deeds might inspire us to similar valor."

Remeya didn't think so, but she didn't voice her opinion.

Lady Corenna liked the notion, her plump face losing its worried cast for a moment.

"Better appreciating the glories of the past than moping about and pulling Aoife down with us," she'd agreed.

So they'd come to this high bridge of a corridor, with its decorative niches and pilasters in one sandstone wall and a series of clear-paned windows on the other. Statues in white marble, in black marble, and creamy golden marble punctuated the long passage, gleaming softly in the pellucid morning sunshine.

Remeya lagged behind while the ladies clustered around the first Imprecatur, carved in gray black and brandishing his great battle axe, *Vahtayvan*. He was depicted in the legionary armor of his time—hardened leather breastplate, leather greaves on his limbs, and a skirt of leather panels protecting his thighs.

Lady Juneya extolled his loyalty and his mighty voice, qualities that saved the people of Istria in his day.

Remeya listened without really hearing and wondered about his faith. He'd lived long before the development of the *pensare* disciplines, hadn't he? Which meant he must have subscribed to the Gedier beliefs. Had *he* prayed before his final battle? Had it helped him?

Lady Corenna, catching sight of the next statue, a cloaked matron in creamy rose marble, scurried forward.

"Oh! The Exemplar Alcea! She could inspire us, if anyone could!"

Remeya lagged further behind. This high corridor was familiar to her. Why had she come here now? To oblige the Lady Juneya? Because she wanted to remember the leap frog games she'd once played beside the statuary with the other castel children?

The ladies moved on from the cloaked and hooded Alcea to a magnificent pegasus done in dazzling white. They ignored a smaller figure cast in bronze and tucked into a wall niche. Did they even notice it?

Ah! *This* was why Remeya was here. Saint Cathal, bent in prayer before his ordeal. What a strange expression the sculptor had given his face: drawn cheeks of fear, set lips of determination, but peace and serenity in his eyes.

Remeya dropped to her knees.

The stone floor was hard and cold through the silks of her chemise and gown. There was a reason for the kneeling bolsters in the chapel!

"Blessed Cathal, save her!" Remeya meant the princess, of course. "Surely your own sacrifice is enough. Your own epistles urge us to live our sacrifices rather than dying them. Please!"

She was aware of the ladies, farther along the gallery and exclaiming over the handsomeness of the beggar's son and the beauty of Ravessa, the Imprecatress who rode across all the continent bringing a cure for plague.

The ladies' footfalls echoed softly, and their voices murmured, fading as they moved away.

Remeya prayed on, even when words failed her and her prayer became one of feeling alone. A sense of comfort stole into her heart. All shall be well, and all shall be well, and all shall be very well, indeed, my love.

Who was telling her of the wholeness in the depths of being? Was it Cathal? Was it Cummenos himself? And *how* would all be well?

The ladies reached the end of the gallery and filed around the corner there, doubtless seeking the spiral stair down to the courtyard far below.

Remeya contemplated the strange contentment pervading her. Nothing had changed, but she felt calmer.

A faint scent of cloves—her father's potpourri—came on her next in-breath and a firm hand touched her shoulder.

"Remeya."

She looked up. "Papere."

He stood beside her in the old-fashioned robes he preferred, a long chemise of sage green, long tunic of pine green, and surcoat of dark umber. She'd not known he was old-fashioned until she'd gone to court and seen the short doublets, padded trunk hose, and striped lower hose worn by the lords there.

"Must you pray so publicly, child?" He sounded exasperated. "Now of all times—"

She felt the too-usual anger of dealing with her father rising in her. "Papere! Now, of all times, are my prayers most needed. Aeliana—*Aoife*—faces death!"

"Must you then risk your own neck?" He was just as irritated as before in his dealings with her. Couldn't they borrow the cordiality of their letters? It seemed not.

She lifted her chin—not far—and stared her father straight in the eye. "Maybe!"

He looked silently back. Then his mouth quirked in a slight, sad smile.

"Besides, they wouldn't—I'm not royal—they—"

"Remeya, you know 'they' are irrelevant. 'He' is the one who might notice. And act."

"But—"

"Is this wise? Reverencing the Holy Hermit? Making the sign of your Horned Lord? Praying at all times and in all places? Think, child! What provoked our king to wrath at the very start of his sojourn in Baloron?"

Remeya bit her lip. "It wasn't little Benne's fault."

"No. But it was his doing." Papere's tone gentled.

"Papere, I'm scared," she admitted.

"You have reason." He touched her wrist, guiding her over to one of the clear, clear windows. In the courtyard below, stable boys led horses out to a dozen armsmen, while three pages hurried in three different directions, bearing messages to various parts of the fortress.

"I visited the High Holy Hind."

Her father shook his head, but the softened lines of his face did not grow stern.

"She told me to pray, and I didn't want to."

"Then, why—?"

"I couldn't think of anything else to do!" she burst out. "Can you?"

He sighed. "No, child. I cannot."

She straightened. "Praying is the only thing left. And Maxim thinks I should."

"Maximo de Pellucon? He's no Gedier."

"No, he isn't," she agreed. "But . . ."

"But what, Remeya?"

She looked down, scuffed one slipper against the smooth red floor, then met her father's gaze again. "He said something about doing what you know is right, what you've practiced, even when it doesn't seem to do anything at all." She felt her lips firm against one another. "This is what I know is right. And"—she regained the contentment interrupted by her father—"I do feel the better for it."

She paused. "Sometimes." Because—in honesty—sometimes she didn't.

Papere's smile grew a little. "So like your mother," he murmured.

"Really?"

He never talked about her mother. All Remeya knew of her came from Nurse. And even Nurse never said much. Perhaps for the same reason? Speaking of Mamere made her too sad?

"Did you know your mother was an old believer?" he asked abruptly.

"No!" There was a jolt. Remeya had wondered. Nurse had been Mamere's nurse too. When Mamere was a child, had Nurse . . . ?

"Yes." Papere brushed her cheek with his forefinger. "And you are like her. Very like."

"Oh! Papere, would you tell me about her? A little?"

He drew a small, flat box from inside his surcoat. It was about the size of his palm and ornamented with minute diamond-shaped tiles of malachite and lapis lazuli. Two delicate gold hinges fastened one side, while a light clasp of gold held the other.

"I carry her portrait. Now."

"Because I'm not here in Baloron, because I bide at court," she guessed, not really understanding why.

A little more light came into his face. He cupped her chin with his hand and leaned forward to kiss her cheek. "Yes."

"But why?"

"Why now?"

She nodded.

He swallowed, shifting his shoulders in a determined way. Another waft of clove potpourri drifted faintly from his robes. He used sachets of it in his clothing chests to keep the moths at bay.

His face firmed.

"I made a very great mistake when your mother died. I avoided all that reminded me of her. Even you. Especially you."

Remeya's breath caught. He'd never been so frank, not even in his letters. There was pain in hearing his admission, and yet a queer relief as well.

"When you departed for Cincrestes, I'd thought the last vestige of my grief left with you. That I'd found peace at last."

That did hurt to hear. That he'd been *glad* for her absence. She stepped away from him. He caught her hands to check her.

"I was wrong. Very wrong."

She waited.

"Only when you were gone did I realize that your resemblance to your mother was a gift. Missing you, I missed her more, not less." Remembered pain creased his eyelids. "All those years I wasted, when I might have cherished you instead of—"

He shook his head. "Instead of guarding myself."

Remeya felt a great stillness within herself, as though a breeze—one so soft and so constant you rarely noticed it—had ceased entirely. She'd assumed her father indifferent, perhaps disliking children. Assumed the growing warmth in his letters to be due to her advancing years.

"Papere," she whispered.

"I love you, my daughter."

Next instant, she was in his arms, embraced, beloved. It felt strange.

After a moment, he released her.

"Can you forgive me, child?" His eyes were curiously humble.

"I don't know." That sounded so cold, but she scarcely knew that she blamed him. Although she sensed she would, given time. But forgiveness before judgment felt impossible.

"Papere, I love you too, but, but . . ."

"This is all new to you."

"Yes."

He smiled, unfamiliarly tender. "Would you like to see your mother's likeness?"

"Please."

He released the clasp holding the panel painting closed. Within, a woman with a cloud of dark curling hair gazed lovingly at the infant she held in her arms.

"Oh!" To see the softly flushed cheek, the glowing eye, and the strong hands of her mother healed something inside her that Remeya had never realized was broken. "Is that me?"

"It is. You were a beautiful infant."

Remeya scrutinized the baby more closely. Really, there wasn't much to see: a closely swaddled scrap of a thing, gazing up at Mamere with large, light-filled eyes.

Remeya returned to studying her mother. Her cheek bones curved more prominently than did Remeya's own, and her lips seemed fuller, but there was reason in Papere's perception that mother and daughter were very like.

"Did Mamere pray?"

A short laugh puffed from her father. "Of course."

"I thought so!"

"But, child, be a little discrete, I beg you."

"Papere, I *am* a Gedier and I revere our Horned Lord." Somehow it seemed important to make him acknowledge it. Acknowledge her as she was. Not the perfect daughter of an imagined past in which he'd comforted rather than ignored. Not the perfect daughter of an imagined future in which he encountered her rarely. But Remeya herself, real and unpredictable.

"I am *me*, Papere!"

"I know you are." He laughed again. "And glad of it."

With his acceptance, spoken aloud, she felt her resistance melt. Perhaps prudence would be possible. Had Aoife been more prudent, would she now face execution? Had little Benne's mamere been prudent . . . ?

Yes, she would be prudent. This new resolve felt good, just as good as her intention to keep praying, but into her fresh contentment another trickle of worry spilled.

"Oh, Papere! Will we lose Baloron?"

She felt almost foolish for caring. It was improbable that Baloron would ever be her dwelling place again. Girls of her station didn't return home. She knew this. And, yet, she cared. Cared fiercely.

Papere took her hand in his, firm and warm and comforting.

"The king has not yet spoken his decision yet. Perhaps—" He glanced down at her. Was that a slight twinkle in his eye? How could he—

"—perhaps you might pray about it."

"Papere!" She heard outrage in her voice, and then she laughed too. "Very well, I *will* pray. For Aoife, for our future. And for home."

"Good girl. But discretely, eh?"

She raised her chin. "As I feel called," she insisted.

And, yet, the strange thing was that discretion imbued her impulse toward devotion in the weeks that followed. In solitude, in the watches of the night or the quiet of a deserted passageway, she prayed. Never in company or before meals. But often with Aoife.

✝

Through all the waiting for the day of his sister's execution, Xavo kept his court lingering at Castel Baloron. Why did they not return to Cincrestes in the capital?

Then King Sevran's battalions arrived and spread in a crescent below the curtain walls. Lord Rollo had been beloved by Sevran, more son than nephew and heir, and his death must be punished.

Had Xavo known of his neighbor's march? Perhaps he was not so oblivious as Maxim's Lord Graezon had feared. Baloron was more defensible than Cincrestes.

Would military necessities prevent Aoife's beheading? Remeya hoped, but no word of such was spoken. Xavo's battle lord tuned the ballistas, while the armsmen drilled in the bailey, and his knights sortied at dawn to trouble Sevran's forces.

With the lake beside their camp, the Eirdrean battalions possessed ample water and game. Sevran could afford to be patient.

Xavo was less fortunate.

The sky tumbled with gray clouds, but the winter rains delayed. The cistern under the inner court stayed bone dry, the spring trickling down the slope of the outer bailey slowed, and the well above it grew shallow and murky. The drought was typical of the season; only the lack of access to the lake made it critical. But towers of cumulous built and built above. The deluge would come soon.

Sevran's trebuchets arrived.

Xavo ordered the cistern filled from the dirty bailey well. From dawn to dusk the castel churls carried buckets to and fro, ceasing only when Sevran's massive war machines were positioned for use and reconfigured from traveling compression to siege array. The last bucket carriers scurried for the shelter of the inner walls as the first slung boulder thudded too close beside their water source.

Sevran's men mined the cliffs of the western lake shore for larger missiles to add to the spiked iron balls brought by the munitions battalion. Bombardment was sporadic, smashing against the curtain walls erratically, bouncing into the dust within the curtain walls less often.

The ballistas atop Baloron's towers answered, and the cries of the wounded went up from both sides.

Atop Tower Nuvolat, the guillotine also went up. Aoife's execution would go forward according to Xavo's decree.

Winter's first storm broke the day before Aoife would be brought to the blade. Rain fell in sheets, filling the cistern to overflowing by midnight and washing the stones of the inner court clean. Sevran's trebuchets ceased lobbing missiles, their balance knocked awry by the mud.

That evening the princess sent her retinue from her side.

"I shall not be alone," she told them, a faint smile flickering in her serene eyes. "The spirit of our Lord—Cummenos manifested as Gwirionedd—accompanies me when you do not. I seek his solace now. In solitude."

Her ladies obeyed her. How could they not? But Remeya was not the only one to grumble. Although Remeya did her grumbling in the privacy of thought, not aloud.

Aoife might be so spiritual that spiritual comfort sufficed *her*. Especially in the exaltation of making such an announcement. But how would she feel in the dark watches of the night, waiting in her cold, somber tower for morning and death? Even if the presence of Cummenos did sustain her, it wouldn't offer much consolation to her ladies, many of whom did not follow the Horned Lord. And those who did . . . well, *Remeya* was not consoled.

The contentment that had visited Remeya sporadically in prayer was vanished now. She felt tense and unhappy and let down, tossing under the coverlet of her bed from the time she climbed into it until the first chill light of dawn brought her tumbling out of it.

The water in her bedside carafe tasted flat and tepid, but she swallowed it anyway, rinsing the dryness from her mouth, almost relieved to have the dreaded morning arrive.

A knock sounded on her chamber door.

A reprieve? Better news? She didn't know why such happy possibilities teased her.

The drooping face of the page boy in the corridor banished them.

"Her Royal Highness bids you attend her," he recited.

The relief of the summons—why was she so relieved?—weakened her knees.

"Thank you!" she gasped, and barely got the door shut before scrambling into yesterday's clothes, still draped over the chest under the window. She'd feared that her last glimpse of Aoife would indeed be her *last* one.

I'm not ready to lose her, not ready at all. Could she ever be? Wouldn't she always need more time? Wouldn't anyone?

Baloron's passageways lay dim and quiet in the dawn, almost normal, as she followed the page through their lonely stretches. Why did she sense a subdued bustle beneath their silence?

Outside, the air flowed cool and fresh, the rain subdued after yesterday's downpour to a gentle misting. Lightning still leaped between the roiling masses of cloud overhead. Remeya pulled the hood of her surcoat well forward.

Ushered into the royal bower of Tower Nuvolat,

she stopped in surprise. Banks of votive candles covered every horizontal surface: the deep and narrow sills of the glazed-in arrow slits; the tops of the old-fashioned flat chests; the spare, bare wood benches and stools; even the flagstone floor, along the walls and in the corners. The round chamber shone, ablaze with light, as though it were the heart of a giant's lantern.

Perhaps Aoife had indeed passed the night watches in religious ecstasy rather than lonely terror.

Remeya had envisioned something very different: the tower as she'd known it during the long weeks of the princess' imprisonment.

For Nuvolat, alone of all Baloron's fortifications was not built of the soft read sandstone native to the area. Centuries ago, in the time of Ravessa, when the serfs dug the pit for the tower's foundations, they'd discovered a vast boulder of iron gray rock. The court astronomer declared it a fallen star. The Gedier priests thought it the remains of a battle mace flung by Cummenos himself. But the castel warder—one of Remeya's ancestors—knew it to be a gift: an igneous stone more durable than most and emplaced to supply the building of Nuvolat without a journey from the distant quarry.

Thus the tower rose dark and ominous amidst Baloron's warm hues.

Nor was the bower within more welcoming. Unused since the days of Xavo's great-grande-mere, the furniture was uncomfortable, devoid of modern cushions. The arrow slits—although furbished with glass—had not been widened and admitted little daylight. While the tapestries—incongruously depicting the mythic journey of the sacred virgin to the Horned Lord's kiss—numbered too few to hide the cold, black, stone walls.

The golden flickering from the hundreds of candles, fragrant with the faint sweetness of beeswax, transformed a chill and cheerless chamber into a chapel, a holy refuge.

Nor was Aoife alone.

Orloitha—present in Baloron as the daughter of Cavalier Erastis, not as the High Holy Hind—stood before the kneeling princess in the Gedier rite of the laying on of hands.

The priestess' Gedier office could never have gained her access to Nuvolat, but she was wielding its powers nonetheless, blessing Aoife's head in the beginning invocation of the ritual.

"Be thou blessed, be thou whole, be thou holy, that Gwirionedd's truth fountain through thy being."

Her voice soothed, low and joyful.

Over Aoife's head, she nodded, welcoming Remeya in.

The guard closed the heavy, bronze-bound door behind her. The candle flames lengthened, reaching upward with the change in the flow of air.

Why did it feel both imprisoning—shutting her away from the life of Baloron—and like arriving within sanctuary after a long journey through rough weather? It made no sense.

Remeya put off her damp surcoat, looked bemusedly for a chest on which to drape it—not a one free of burning candles—and folded it over her arm. The quilted silk felt sticky against her skin.

She moved to kneel by the princess, sharing the other end of her long prayer bolster.

Aoife glanced aside at her from beneath Orloitha's outstretched fingers and said abruptly: "I think you cannot know my whole heart, Remeya, and I fear that lack might hurt you in time. I wish to remedy your future while I yet may."

Remeya crinkled her brow. This made as little sense as the strange illusion that she'd been condemned along with Aoife and the still stranger one that she'd reached sanctuary and been relieved of the weight of the outer world. What did the princess mean?

"Your Highness, you owe me nothing."

"Indeed, I owe you much. Truly." Aoife drew in a breath. " Please hear me."

Orloitha's hands moved from the top of Aoife's head to her brow.

"Be thou seeing, be thou just, be thou unwavering, that Eoin's judgment inform thy discernment."

Remeya shifted, pulling her gown smooth where it creased uncomfortably between her knee and the firm bolster. She stared earnestly at Aoife.

"Your Highness, I will hear you, of course, if it will comfort you, but—"

Aoife smiled, a lovely warm relaxation of her face that had been tense for so many months. "Thank you." She placed a hand, cool and light, on Remeya's, clasped against her waist. "I think you have taken responsibility for saving me, have you not?"

Remeya's eyes widened. "Yes. Yes, I did. But, how—?"

A low, rippling laugh broke from Aoife. "Ah, child, your low spirits and disapproving face told me as much. How could it be otherwise whilst your heart bade me have prudence and my own urged me to forego it?"

A flushing warmth passed through Remeya's chest. Who was she to judge a princess? Yet she had. And Aoife knew it.

"I beg your pardon, Highness."

Aoife laughed again, then grew solemn. "No. I must beg yours."

"Oh! No, indeed, your Highness!"

"Yes, indeed." The liveliness in Aoife's voice reminded Remeya vividly of her first year under the princess' aegis, when Xavo and his sister had bantered one another and entertained their court with games and humor. The brightness of it, so merry and innocent against the present darkness, stabbed her.

Aoife squeezed Remeya's hands, then let them go.

"I am not sure I can make you understand, but I must try." She paused, her lips straightening. "Did you know that my brother shared my Gedier faith when we were small?"

Remeya's eyes grew large again. No, she hadn't. She shook her head.

"Our father bade him embrace the *pensare* when he invested him as heir to the rule of Istria, and Xavo obeyed. But his renounced beliefs make him both secretly sympathetic to mine and, equally, troubled by them."

Orloitha moved her hands to Aoife's throat. "Be thou speaking, be thou true, be thou clarion, that Cummenos doth move in thee and in the world."

Aoife's gaze traveled from Remeya to the Holy Hind.

A flash of joy illumined her face and was reflected in Orloitha's.

Then the princess returned to her narrative. "When Xavo lost himself"—when he claimed the falchion, she meant, there on the hillside by the spring—"I knew the balance between his conscience and his tolerance might shift."

A sudden rush of guilt mingled with questions crowded Remeya's chest, but she stifled her speech. Aoife had asked this interval to clear her conscience, and she deserved it. Remeya would not encroach on it with her own concerns.

The princess continued. "As Xavo changed, he confirmed my fears, and I pondered how I would act." She bit her lip. "Remeya, you are my fosterling and, as such, have a special claim on me. To you I owed my self-preservation. 'Tis unfair to make a commitment to a child and then break it."

Remeya's hands gripped one another, knuckles whitening. "Your Highness—"

Aoife interrupted her. "And, Remeya, I am breaking it. Do not deny it."

Remeya wanted to, but wasn't this what she'd been telling herself ever since they'd come to Baloron? Not so much that Aoife owed *her*, but that Aoife owed *all* those who loved her some degree of prudence. "But you could not deny Our Horned Lord."

Aoife sighed. "No. I could not. And that *is* what my brother required of me."

Now Remeya reached out to clasp Aoife's hand. "Your Highness, I knew this without your telling me."

"Did you?" Aoife's eyes turned shrewd. "Really? In your heart?"

Remeya swallowed. "I knew it. I just didn't want it to be true."

"Then know this also: you are not responsible for my choices. Or for my brother's. Only for your own."

Yes. Therein lay the problem. She didn't like her own. And she'd been trying to like them better by judging Aoife for hers. It hadn't worked.

Was this why Aoife had summoned her? To teach her this?

The princess brushed the back of a finger across Remeya's cheek. "Thou art strong," she murmured.

Orloitha touched the princess' solar plexus. "Be thou living, be thou warm, be thou pliant, that Our Ternion Lord doth breathe in thee."

The door behind them opened, admitting booted footsteps.

Startled, Remeya glanced over her shoulder.

Lords Ezek and Merral paused just over the threshold, gazing askance at the massed candles and the two women engaged in a Gedier ritual.

A sudden dash of rain spatted against one of the narrow windows. Thunder grumbled.

"Your Royal Highness, it is time." Lord Merral's voice emerged low, barely audible. Was he ashamed?

"Thou shalt bide until I hath completed Our Lord's blessing." Orloitha sounded unconcerned.

Lord Merral looked at Lord Ezek. Lord Ezek looked at Lord Merral.

Remeya would have laughed were it not for the panic rising in her breast. *Not now! Not now! Not now!*

Clearly the two men did not have the mandate to wait. Equally clearly they were going to do so anyway.

Orloitha carried on serenely, blessing the remaining sacred points: the belly in honor of Cummenos' hunger; the loins, holy by Eoin's reverence for fertility; and the root, where Gwirionedd's breath becomes physicality incarnate.

Lord Ezek tapped his foot anxiously.

Orloitha glanced up sharply.

Lord Ezek stilled his foot.

Then Orloitha was done.

She rose, supporting the princess as Aoife also regained her feet. Remeya lagged behind them. If she just stayed kneeling, would time stop?

Another growl of thunder sounded. Another spat of rain slapped the window glass.

Orloitha fetched garments from the princess' sleeping couch, the only furnishing unburdened by candles.

Remeya held the princess' surcoat—flame orange in celebration of Cummenos' autumn chase—while Orloitha helped Aoife to pull a scarlet tabard over her gown. As she accepted her surcoat from Remeya's hands, she smiled down at her. "Bide here, child. I would not have you witness it."

Remeya gulped. What did one say to one's foster mother approaching her death?

Abruptly, she threw her arms around Aoife and buried her face in her shoulder. "I'll miss you! Oh, I'll miss you!" she cried.

Aoife smiled, sadness tingeing the strange joy on her lips. "Fare thee well."

Then the Lords Ezek and Merral were flanking the princess, escorting her out of the bower and up the stone stairs curving along the tower wall.

✝

"Come!" Orloitha gestured Remeya.

"Oh, but—! Aoife said—"

"What dost thy heart say?"

Don't go! Go!

I want no part of this. I *am* a part of this!

Please stay. I cannot stay away!

She passed under the bower archway and, side by side with Orloitha, followed in the princess' wake—climbing Tower Nuvolat, climbing toward a blade, climbing into a dreaded future.

They stepped through a door at the top of the spiral steps onto a small landing at the bottom of a short, narrow straight stairwell. Stone walls enclosed it, but no vaulting concealed the gray and hurrying sky.

The rain had slackened once more, but the steps were wet and slippery. Remeya forgot to put her hood up. The misty air, cool against her cheeks, smelled so fresh and clean. How could it with such horror ahead?

Dying thunder growled. Was there a murmur behind the sky's mutter? Gulls blown astray on the wind? The roars of an aurochs stung by a refugée hedgehog? Or the hounds in the mews, weary of neglect and defying the tumult of last night's storm?

Aoife and her escort had slowed. Remeya nearly trod

on their heels as they took the last step and emerged on the rooftop.

Nuvolat was tall, so tall. Its high circular terrace, bounded with the crenellations of massive battlements, seemed more a place of wind and clouds and sky than of earth. Far below, the matted grasses and brambles of the outer bailey sloped away to Baloron's curtain wall, dark with wet and half hidden in the mists. The lake, with King Sevran's sullen encampment, appeared a mere black blot in the distance.

But all Remeya's attention focused on what awaited them here atop the tower.

King Xavo, cloaked in somber blue, stood between the Lords Pernice and Lazelo on his left and the executioner on his right.

The king's face threatened death, but not more so than the guillotine beside the group of men. A wicked scaffolding of heavy timber braced the sharp, slanted blade of bronze suspended within its framework.

A kneeling bolster—bright orange brocade—rested on the flagstones in front of the apparatus.

Oh, god! Oh, god!

Lord Ezek clipped Aoife's hair to jaw length. Lord Merral helped her remove her surcoat and its neck-engulfing hood. Orloitha kissed her on the cheek.

Aoife's joy had fallen from her. She seemed calm, but pale. How could she be calm? Remeya was anything but calm.

The princess crossed the terrace to the guillotine and knelt on the cushion provided.

Thunder grumbled again, louder this time.

The cries of—what creature was that? hounds surely—clashed with the storm's voice. But they came from above, not below. Hounds in the sky?

A yet louder barrage of thunder boomed, and a rider galloped from a misting gap between low clouds. A sky-borne rider amidst hounds.

He was larger than Baloron's gatehouse, terrible in his power, dark against the roiling heavens.

Remeya flinched away, unable to bear sight of him, animal and huge as his steed pounded across shaking, riven air.

Nor was she alone in her fear.

Xavo himself turned his head down over a shoulder, and the courtiers flung themselves prone. Of all gathered on the stone roof, only Orloitha stood fast, tipping her face up and flinging her arms aloft. "Brenin gwyllt!"—wild lord—"Glanhau y budreddi!"—cleanse this putrescence!

The rider bowed his head, a stag's head crowned by its weighty rack. Remeya looked away again.

Why do they call him the Horned One? He bears antlers, not horns.

Cummenos' hounds gave tongue, clamorous and fell. The sky cracked, shaking the tower with a force as great as any trebuchet, and lightning stabbed down.

The guillotine splintered, up and not out, spurting like a fountain, leaving Aoife untouched.

Remeya's knees trembled. She peeked at the king. He cowered still, but his right hand crept along his thigh, feeling for his weapon. Did he dream of challenging this foe? Battling the Lord of the Wild Hunt in a final, apocalyptic duel? Defeating the Gedier deity? Making Istrian *pensare* pre-eminent once and for all?

No.

Abruptly she knew. His aim was nothing so lofty. The blade to sever his sister's head from her body was broken. He would wield this blade instead!

Would no one stop him?

Lord Merral? Lord Ezek? Cummenos' High Holy Hind?

The courtiers had scuttled for the trap door. Xavo's executioner gripped his ceremonial axe as though he would fall without its support. Orloitha channeled her god's awe, face upraised, eyes shut.

In the recent habit of prayer, Remeya prayed once more. "Brenin gwyllt! Save her!"

And then she knew.

I must save her, if saved she is to be.

Remeya's limbs felt like cold clay absent any animating force. The aura of Cummenos beat against her like a mighty river's cascade, too powerful to permit movement. She stood frozen in place.

The king's hand crept closer to the falchion's grip.

Remeya exerted her will, determined to lunge, to reach, to grasp, but her body stayed still. Willpower was not enough. Could prayer do ought . . . ?

"Brenin gwyllt, help *me*!"

Remeya seemed to glide in slow motion, weighted by the terrible glance of the Horned One and the bellowing of his hounds. Her hand, gelid *longing* pressing cold droplets from dense ice, floated forward yet more slowly.

But she was faster than Xavo.

Her fingers slid around the grip ahead of his, pried the falchion from the scabbard, and withdrew it from the king's closing fist.

Remeya gasped.

Pain bloomed deep in her joints, curling her downward, twisting her clutching fingers awry, dragging her eyelids down over darkening sight. She shuddered, gulping and fighting to stay upright.

At the corner of her vision, she saw Xavo beginning his own lunge, his visage savage, his hand thrusting forward, his purpose—the retrieval of his falchion—clear.

Remeya sobbed, still pinned by pain. *He'll take it from me in my weakness!*

She shuffled a step away from the king. Even in her clumsiness, she was quicker than he. It was as though time itself weighed his limbs down while buoying hers.

The pain in her joints sharpened, stabbing so fiercely that she almost expected to see herself dismembered, each bone falling to the stones unattached. Then the agony ebbed completely, giving way to a surge of strength accompanied by disorientation.

"Brenin gwyllt?" she whispered in confusion.

The strength bearing her up seemed to thrum in her bones and in her ears.

I am one of Cummenos' pack, a hound to hunt evil from the land.

She gripped the falchion more tightly, shifting her weight to spin and take the king's head as he had planned to take his sister's.

I'll avenge her!

Remeya spun. She slashed.

And somewhere beneath the thrumming strength possessing her, another voice spoke within her, still and small. *No! Your king requires salvation also.*

Somehow Remeya pulled the blow, missing the king by a hair's breadth.

And yet her thoughts were not freed from their distortions. She knew the executioner deserved death for following his king's orders blindly; the courtiers for their cowardice; the High Holy Hind for allowing her religious exultation to remove her from the matter at hand; and the princess for her lethal honesty.

I'll kill them all!

Beneath her bloodlust, the still small voice spoke again: *Pray, Remeya! Pray!*

She fell to her knees, wondering that she could do so, wondering that the quieter voice could overpower the shouting one that demanded death.

With the intention to pray came a moment of peace, a moment of freedom. She had choice in that moment. She could pray as she had never prayed before, or she could hold something back—as she'd always done before—and lose . . . everything.

"Brenin gwyllt," she whispered, "I am yours."

"Fod yn gryf, calon dewr!"—*Be strong, brave heart!* The god's voice was a buffet, stripping her of all her unnatural strength, and yet . . . stripping her of its compulsion also.

Was *this* the purpose of prayer? Not only to make oneself ready when the moment of opportunity arrived, but to draw ever nearer to one's god? Was this what Aoife had meant when she said *give* yourself *to him*?

Remeya surged to her feet, stiffening her knees. Then she bent most deliberately, lowering the falchion toward her heels. With heart alone impelling her arms—all her strength still fled—she flung the blade skyward.

Up, up, her gaze followed its flight.

The Lord of the Hunt reached out his mighty hand, grasped the falchion, strangely larger, and brandished it in appalling strokes.

Could a god go mad? As had the king? As had Remeya herself in the falchion's thrall?

No, his blows were well placed, his steed and hounds in no danger.

He sliced a portal in the sky above his rack and tossed the falchion through it, up again, into vapor and wind.

It was gone.

The hounds belled. The horseman called. And the hunt swept over Tower Nuvolat, pounding through another rent in the violent clouds, hidden by the mists.

Remeya listened.

The wild call of the hounds moved across the

sky behind the clouds, punctuated by the cries of the huntsman. Did triumph ring in their fell voices?

Distance muted the clamor of the hunt, then silenced it.

✝

Remeya lowered her gaze from the heavens.

Orloitha stood rapt, eyes closed. The executioner gripped his pole axe, mouth open and eyes wide. The courtiers had fled. The only others remaining on the battlement were the princess and the king.

Aoife knelt still, but her back was straight and her head flung back.

Xavo fell to his knees before her, crunching down on the shards of the guillotine, heedless of sharp metal and splinters. He spoke steadily, but tears glided down his lean cheeks. "I am not fit. My deeds prove it. Whilst thou wear my crown, sister?"

She shook her head, smiling.

"I beg thee," he pressed her.

"'Twas not thee, brother," she said, "but the blade. The Wild Lord hath accepted it. Thou art free of its taint."

He bowed his head. "Canst thou forgive me?" he whispered.

"I have."

He reached for her, tentatively, then drew her into his embrace when she accepted his touch. This time he did sob. She stroked his hair.

"Ask me a boon!" he commanded, raising his face.

Her voice was tender. "Thou knowest my desire."

"It is thine," he declared. "The Gedier shall be received in my court, welcomed by my counselors, and adjudged safe under my law."

Now tears spangled Aoife's cheeks. "Blessed be, dear brother. Blessed be."

"How canst thou forgive me?" His voice broke. "*I* cannot!"

"I rejoice in thy return," she answered simply.

The proclamation reinstating the Gedier had to be done all over again in the great hall before the assembled lords and ladies, armsmen, and bishops of the *pensare*. But before the king issued orders for that gathering, before even his sister sent messages to the castel cooks to prepare the feast that would follow it, Xavo commanded his heralds to approach King Sevran under the white flag of truce to sue for peace.

"I have been wrong and doubly wrong, but I need not compound my error with the losses of war. Whatever he demands, I shall pay it!" he declared.

But Sevran, too, had suffered a change of heart.

Had the Horned Lord shattered everyone within sight of him, within hearing of his mighty voice?

Xavo's heralds met Sevran's approaching the curtain walls when they emerged through the great gate of Baloron's outer bailey, and soon the two kings stood on the hillside by the old well, talking and gesturing and, finally, embracing. Sevran begged Aoife's hand in marriage at the close of the negotiation.

She accepted.

Through all these doings, Remeya stood on the fringes of the actors, feeling very strange indeed.

The princess was saved. What a joyous event. She should feel happy.

The princess was saved through Remeya's own hand. She should feel light, her atonement for her retrieval of the falchion complete.

War was averted. Her own Horned Lord had made his presence felt, unmistakably so. She should be ecstatic.

Instead she felt . . . how did she feel?

Emptied out. Inutterably weary. All purpose fled.

She stood blankly on the hillside in the misting rain with the others—the ladies-in-waiting, the nobles of the king's court, the heralds, and the banner carriers— waiting to attend the princess, should the princess call upon her.

But Aoife didn't call her. At her brother's side, on his arm, her glance meeting his, she was attended by him, bright with her joy. And then attended by her betrothed.

The ladies twittered and fluttered, aflow with the romance of it all.

The courtiers smiled and bowed, satisfied that the siege was over and with little cost to them.

Remeya smelled the fresh scent of the washed air along with the earthy odor of the damp silks of the court. The two kings' voices seemed to hold all enthralled, a resonant current moving from serious, somber tones to glad-ringing laughs, and bringing contentment to all save Remeya.

Why did she feel as though her efforts, her very life energy, had been . . . squandered?

Surely not!

And yet she did.

Did victory always feel like this? Anti-climactic?

But imagine if she were grieving loss now instead of triumph. *Was* she grieving loss?

Grieving?

Yes, she was. How odd.

Her strange sense of moving in isolation persisted even as she joined the entire castel population in the great hall on the second floor of the square central keep.

Gray light poured in through the many tall and modernized mullioned windows. The banners of the lords in attendance—nearly all of them—moved in the draughts reaching the high beams from which the bright fabrics hung. The black wolf on white and tan that was Graezon; the blue falcon against the forest green and crimson of Pellucon; the scarlet lynx over black and white checkers. The king's own royal blue eagle against gold and copper stripes; the princess' sky blue version.

Sevran's heraldry did not keep company amongst them, of course. His squire carried the Eirdrean square of umber brown with its silver dove bearing a golden acorn.

Nerilla, standing beside Remeya in the crowd, nudged her former nursling's elbow when Sevran entered the hall on a fanfare of trumpets. "Oh, isn't he a handsome one, for sure?" she chortled.

Remeya nodded and smiled, but still her sense of aloofness held her apart from the murmuring echoes of voices and footsteps filling the hall; apart from the faint scents of the varied potpourris used to store the garments of the nobility and imbued in their folds: spicy cinnamon, fresh applewood, floral rose; untouched by the vivid pageantry. Her rain-dampened gown and chemise felt sticky against her skin.

I don't belong here.

How could that be? Here in her home, in the hall where her father had spoken many a decree to the castel residents. She *should* belong here. But she didn't.

King Xavo declared the Gedier faith to be legitimate and recognized by the crown.

Nerilla raised her right hand, fingers split in the signed of the Horned Lord. The lords and ladies shared wary glances while the serving staff followed Nerilla's ebullient lead.

The king announced his sister's betrothal to King Sevran, and everyone cheered.

Remeya realized that her voice had joined them in celebrating the news even while her heart stayed cold.

Only when the king tacked an unexpected addendum onto the business of the gathering did she come back to herself, come back to the present moment, limbs solid and thoughts focused.

The warm red of the stone walls glowed more warmly. The shuffling of the crowd rustled louder. The press of her neighbors enfolded her more closely.

What was the king saying?

"Castel Baloron shall belong to the Gedier order henceforth, theirs to tend and defend, theirs to enjoy and flourish within, theirs to strengthen against the peril sequestered in the sky above Tower Novulat."

Blessed Cathal! She had lost her home in a way totally unforeseen.

Xavo believed the falchion to be neither removed nor destroyed—merely hidden beyond the reach of men and women—and he feared it yet, perhaps wisely.

But—but—but!

"I give one last decree for Baloron before I cede it," proclaimed the king. "My faithful Lord Otavo"— Remeya's father—"shall choose if he and his heirs attend Baloron in perpetuity or gain a new keep under his ward: my new Castel Zaphiron abuilding on the hilltop to be my main stronghold."

Remeya held her breath. Could Baloron yet be hers? A haven from which she sailed into her future? Which would her sire choose?

"I bide here, my king, in the home of my ancestors, the home of my legacy."

Oh, relief. Fosterlings rarely returned home again. Especially girls.

But I want to know that home is still there.

Xavo turned toward Orloitha. She was garbed in the celebratory robes of the hart-kin and glowed. "I commend him—my faithful lord—and his to thy respect and affection. I owe his daughter a debt greater than may be repaid. Cherish him and his, I charge thee to pledge thy troth so."

"I do," answered the sacred Hind.

At last Remeya felt happy.

And not a calm, serene happiness either.

She bubbled, she fizzed, and she could not stay still with it.

✝

Leaving the great hall ahead of the crowd, she positively skipped down the massive main staircase and through the series of guardrooms forming the foundations of the keep.

"Whoa there, girlie." That was the stablemaster, grizzled and gray, with a gravelly voice. "Ye dinna want t' tumble doon on your haid."

But she could not hold her excitement in check.

Outside, the clouds had parted to reveal a deep cobalt blue sky. The low sun of evening cast slanting light across the inner bailey, creating soft splotches of dry rose amidst the dark red of the wetter stone. A wide puddle where the paving dipped in front of the gatehouse reflected stone and sky and sun.

Seized by pure silliness, Remeya ran and jumped in it, not caring that the water drenched her beginning-to-dry slippers and spattered the page boys dashing on their errands. They laughed with her. The whole world—her world—was happy.

The banquet hall proved an extension of her mood; hangings of cream and silver and palest copper draped the walls, snowy white linen covered the tables, and a forest of crystal candelabras pointed lighted tapers toward the high, pointed vault of the ribbed ceiling.

The aroma of succulent roast boar—contributed by King Sevran—wafted from the screened passage to the kitchens along with hints of citrus and a thread of honey.

Remeya discovered she was hungry.

Hungry? No, ravenous. She'd merely picked at her food in all the long weeks of Aoife's incarceration.

Her rank and station placed her at the royal table between the Lords Merral and Ezek. She'd rather have been seated by her father. His eyes met hers across the width of the hall. They were smiling, almost hesitantly, as though he couldn't believe his good fortune and yet did, despite the experience that made him wary.

One of his brows shifted upward a fraction.

Was she alright?

She nodded and lifted her goblet of mead. Yes.

Lord Merral teased her about her appetite, but plucked choice viands from the meat platters and tender grapes from the fruit bowl to supplement her own selections. Lord Ezek quoted vulgar poetry to entertain her, about tinkers, gypsies, and pilgrims.

Remeya's spirits grew ever more boisterous until the energy in her overwhelmed her happiness. Restless and unsettled, she pushed back her chair.

"My lady?" Lord Merral, concerned.

"Damoselle?" Lord Ezek, reluctant to lose his laughing audience.

"I seek the air," she excused herself. It wasn't so far from true. The warmth generated by some hundred feasting nobles, the seared meats, and the thousand tapers had heated the hall uncomfortably. But neither was it the truth. Remeya just couldn't bear to sit still.

Both lords presented their upturned palms.

"Let me escort you!"

"Bear me company, damoselle!"

"No! I crave solitude." And she fled, not running, but moving swiftly, to be sure.

Down from the dais, behind the backs of the diners lining one long table and then another, dodging two serving men who carried a peacock made of sugar crystals—turquoise and jade and silver.

She achieved the screened passage and sped for the pair of outside doors.

Delightfully cool evening air caressed her cheek. The first stars sparked in the blue-black bowl of the sky, while a last rim of orange color limned the western horizon. Remeya skirted the broad puddle before the gatehouse this time, passing through that massive block to the middle bailey. A dim silhouette approached in this passage between the middle and outer baileys.

"Lady Remeya?"

His voice, familiar, soothed her ear. Sudden relief rushed through her.

"Max!"

He would help her. Guide her to regain . . . something. Her balance, perhaps.

He offered his arm.

The linen of his sleeve felt soft under her fingertips, his muscles beneath the fabric, firm and reliable.

"You're dressed for travel?" She'd not seen him in the banquet hall, but surely he'd been present for the earlier ceremony in the keep.

"Just a brief jaunt to Cincrestes for his majesty."

"Oh, then—"

"I'm returning, Remeya, not departing."

"Oh!" Another wash of relief assuaged her momentary alarm. "Max—?"

"Hmm?" He guided her out through the farther

archway, continuing in the direction she'd been headed. "Whither, my lady?"

My lady? Not her name? Why the sudden formality?

"My lord?" Her voice trembled.

The slope of the bailey fell away from them, gray in the dusk against the darkening eastern sky. Thin columns of smoke rose up from the cooking fires of Sevran's camp. The Eirdrean king had not neglected his men. They, too, feasted, although distance lent quiet to their no-doubt merry celebrations.

Max's teeth flashed in a sudden grin. "My lady?" he repeated.

"Oh, Max, don't!"

"Remeya, then." He chuckled.

"Yes, please. Take me to the well."

Her slippers, which had dried while she banqueted, grew wet again. The flagstones of the inner court had given up their moisture to the late warmth of the eventide, but the bailey grasses had not. The air hung very still while the last color in the sky faded. More stars pricked out.

The broad stone coping that rimmed the wellhead retained some warmth. Max seated her there and knelt before her, taking her hand in his. The light, steady clasp felt good. Just his presence felt good.

"His Majesty had planned to honor you at the feasting hall, you know. 'Praise her with great praise,' and all that. You escaped too soon."

Her distress, subsiding under his influence, rose up again.

"It has all come right in the end, but there was so much pain and peril—"

He didn't pretend to misunderstand her. "The falchion was evil," he agreed.

"And it was all my fault." She still felt so, but that wasn't it. Wasn't what she wanted to say. Somewhere beneath the fact of her guilt lay another truth. One more difficult to grasp, less simple than guilt and innocence.

The faint scent of woodsmoke drifted from the far lakeside. Did the evening air start to move?

She wasn't sure she could put into words what she needed to, wanted to.

Max's face, dim in the gloaming, looked easily back at her.

"It wasn't what I did. Or it was! But even more than what I did—fetching the falchion from the earth and the water—was my *consent*."

That was it.

"How so, Remeya?" He sounded puzzled. The growing night hid the nuances of his expression from her, but she knew his voice. "Xavo *did* ask it of you."

"But it was mine to say no." She knew that now. Even a king might be denied in chosen moments.

And she had consented to far more than obeying the king's will. She knew that too.

Loosing the falchion on the king and, through him, on all Istria, had been an evil act. But participating in his passion of wrath, in Aoife's passion of integrity, had been even more damaging for her personally. *That* was the truth she was trying to unearth.

"Max, will you teach me the *pensare*?"

She'd learned the disciplines, of course, but she'd not practiced them in years.

Max rocked back on his heels.

"Remeya, the Horned Lord himself called to you. Surely you'll not renounce him now?"

"No, oh, no." And she would not. She felt herself more firmly Gedier than ever—no, more firmly her *god's*—although she suspected her faith would feel the impact of Cummenos' words to her in ways she could not imagine now, and at times that would surprise her in the years ahead. She could hardly take it in—too paramount, too powerful. There was a reason the divine usually spoke more subtly to mere mortals.

But this nearer concern—how she'd adopted the

king's troubles and those of the princess as those of her own—that was something she must deal with now.

She gripped Max's hands and welcomed his answering strength.

"*Pensareans* deny the Horned Lord, but the *pensare* itself does not."

"Yes, that's true." Max shifted forward again, his knee pressing down in the damp turf. "You would become a pensarean Gedier? With my help?"

"You feel so *balanced*, Max. I want that. I *need* that."

She was convinced the *pensare* gave it to him. If she'd been practicing *pensare* postures all along, perhaps she would not have abandoned herself to dwell so completely in the concerns of the royal family. The Gedier embraced feeling. The *pensareans* cultivated serenity. She wanted both.

Max renewed his clasp on her hands. "Will *you* teach *me* the Gedier rites?"

She could hear the smile in his question.

"Really?" Did he truly wish to become one of the hart-kin?

"If you are to become a *pensarean* Gedier, why should not I become a Gedian *pensare* practitioner?" He came off his knee to sit beside her on the well coping. "Will you, sweet Remeya?"

She wanted to embrace him. "I think you deserve a better teacher."

"But you are the teacher I want. Come, Remeya, we'll learn from one another."

She felt shy then.

"I'd like that, Max, but are you sure? I've made so many mistakes." She sighed. "Especially—especially in the last year."

"Xavo has a good bit more to redeem, you know."

"But that's *his* task. Atonement for my sins is mine."

"Yes. It is. But, Remeya, surrendering to guilt is not atonement. Make this your first practice of balance. Remember that while you drew the falchion from its watery grave, so you also cast it aloft where Cummenos himself redeemed your error.

"You cannot claim your sin without also claiming your triumph."

He had a point there. The beginnings of a smile tugged her lips.

"Will you try, Remeya? Commit yourself to reason amidst your emotion?"

Oh, he understood. And understood her.

She raised her chin.

"Yes, I will."

Somehow her promise shifted something. She wasn't

sure what, but she felt . . . clear. Lighter. Happy, but a calm happy this time.

Max leaned in to kiss her cheek.

"Then I'm satisfied."

And so was she.

The night breeze picked up, lifting the tendrils of her hair from around her face.

THE END

Appendices

Ritual Sacrifice

The Gedier faith has its roots in the Stone Age of the North-lands when primitive tribes enacted fertility rites to ensure that the fading winter sun returned to strength and new life in the summer. Each autumn a young man was invested with the divinity of the sun, slain, and buried. His burial ensured that the sun's sacred union with the earth took place, from which the light would rise in the resurrection of spring.

As tribal thinking evolved through the millennia, their religious beliefs also changed and evolved.

By the Bronze Age, the ritual slaying no longer took place every year, but was reserved to commemorate special events or to ward off extraordinary danger.

And, in the Iron Age, human sacrifice was condemned as a barbaric practice not perpetrated by civilized people. In spite of the condemnation, the kings of Istria, Eirdry, and Ennecy—the heart of the lands that would grow into the Giralliyan empire—occasionally sacrificed *themselves* in the old rite to preserve or rescue their subjects from disasters such as draught and famine, pestilence, or war against a mighty enemy.

However, the practice died out entirely for several centuries during the years of classical antiquity.

The religious beliefs of neighboring cultures were added to Gedier philosophy, and the emphasis shifted away from the physical world and its necessities toward the inner world of the individual and the choices made by the individual.

Then, in late antiquity, when unusual prosperity reigned, human sacrifice was revived under the guise of religious ritual but with the true purpose of entertainment for the masses.

The Holy Hermit Cathal was born into the social unrest and turbulence of this time. As a young man he pursued the course of an ascetic, withdrawing from human contact to pursue a life of simplicity and meditation. Later in life, one of the destined human sacrifices escaped to Cathal's lonely hut in the hills and changed Cathal's outlook.

Cathal realized that withdrawing from tumult was cowardly, and he emerged to challenge the disgusting practice of human sacrifice, speaking nearly every day to crowds in the realms of Istria, Eirdry, and Ennecy.

Eventually he was imprisoned by the regime of Istria and sentenced to die in the ritual slaying that he condemned. He was permitted to speak before his slaying, and his words were so eloquent that the onlookers rioted as he was hoisted up to hang head down and receive the ax blow to his chest.

The riots did not end there, and spread across not only the three heartland realms, but across all of Giralliya as his final speech was repeated again and again.

The Gedier faith changed irrevocably, although that was not the end to its challenges.

Five hundred years after Cathal's death, times were more uncertain. Massed troll armies fought in the northern reaches of the continent, driving many tribal peoples south to escape them. The civilized realms were hard pressed; some were overrun.

The Gedier faith was flagging. The new *pensarean* discipline that proved effective against **Beyhalt's** plague was growing in popularity. Many found the *pensare* more effective for procuring inner peace than the rituals of the Gedier.

The heretic Bellam was born into this milieu, the son of a devout Gedier family.

Bellam declared that the reason the troll horde was winning victory after victory on the battlefield was due to the focus on the inner life encouraged by both the *pensare* and the Gedier beliefs as they were currently constituted. He called for a return to the robust practice of human sacrifice.

A vocal minority heeded his call, and within Bellam's sect Istrian soil once again was stained by the blood of innocents.

Bellam was eventually captured and imprisoned, but his followers refused to renounce their gory practices.

The Gedier belief was declared forbidden, and eventually Bellam's sect died out.

The peaceful practitioners continued their worship in secret, however, and the Gedier religion continued to live with varying degrees of tolerance and varying numbers of believers.

The story *Hunting Wild* takes place during one of the many Gedier revivals, but the religion did not survive forever. By the time of the events in *Troll-magic* (800 years later), the Gedier beliefs were not only dead, but forgotten by all but a few scholars of history.

The Ternion God

The Gedier worship a god with three aspects, each aspect with its own name: Gwirionedd, Cummenos, and Eoin.

Gwirionedd is said to preside in paradise, bringing bliss and glory to the souls of the dead. Literal old believers focus on this promise, but the Gedier faith in the time of *Hunting Wild* is oriented toward metaphorical realities rather than literal ones.

Gwirionedd represents that part of divinity that radiates holy light within each believer, guiding him or her to choose lovingly and lifegivingly. More abstractly yet, Gwirionedd blows through all creation like a holy breeze, sustaining the underlying pattern of the world.

In the worship rituals of the Gedier, Gwirionedd is celebrated from the spring equinox to the harvest.

At the harvest, the liturgical year shifts to Cummenos. This aspect of the god is the oldest, going back to the Stone Age tribes who killed their sacral king to ensure that the ever-shortening days of fall would not shorten down to eternal night, but would lengthen again to bring spring and summer.

Cummenos is a warrior god, taking the form of a man with a stag's head. He rides a war horse in the midst of a pack of hounds and hunts evil from the face of the earth: the lingering ghosts of murderers, monsters such as ice wyrms, and the blood drinkers who resist mortality.

More metaphorically, he hunts the destructive essence that hides in the soul of each believer, flushing sin from the shadows and aiding the believer to turn toward hope.

Cummenos is said to chase both monsters and sin in his Wild Hunt down into hell. His aspect is celebrated in worship and ritual from the harvest to the winter solstice.

Then the liturgical year turns to Eoin.

Just as the Gedier god has three aspects, so does Eoin possess two. Although they are superimposed on one another, rather than existing separately.

Eoin the Judge is both a man with compassionate eyes and a satyr: with the hind legs of a goat, a man's torso and arms, and a goat's head with curling goat's horns.

Literally, he judges each soul at the moment of death, discerning the death-wishing elements within and whether they may be transformed or must be discarded. And, if the latter, whether there is enough left to be translated to paradise.

Spiritually, Eoin helps each believer work with the process of self transformation, strengthening virtues and lessening flaws.

Eoin's aspect is celebrated from the winter solstice to the spring equinox. And then the liturgical year returns to Gwirionedd to start the cycle of worship again.

Timeline for the North-lands Stories

ANCIENT TIMES

Skies of Navarys — 3000 years before *Troll-magic*

THE WARRING EPOCH

The Smith and the Hermit — 2500 years before *Troll-magic*

Blood Falchion — 200 years after *The Smith and the Hermit*

The Kite Climber — 400 years after *The Smith and the Hermit*

To Haunt the Daring Place — 450 years after
The Smith and the Hermit

THE BRONZE AGE

The Tally Master — *2000 years before Troll-magic*

Sovereign Night — 18 months after *The Tally Master*

Resonant Bronze — ~8 years after *Sovereign Night*

THE MIDDLE AGES

Hunting Wild — 800 years before *Troll-magic*

BEFORE THE STEAM AGE

Rainbow's Lodestone — ~100 years before *Troll-magic*

Star-drake — immediately after *Rainbow's Lodestone*

THE STEAM AGE

Sarvet's Wanderyar — 52 years before *Troll-magic*

Crossing the Naiad — concurrent with *Sarvet's Wanderyar*

Livli's Gift — 38 years after *Sarvet's Wanderyar*

(14 years before *Troll-magic*)

Troll-magic — the "now" of this timeline

The Troll's Belt — contemporaneous with *Troll-magic*

Perilous Chance — contemporaneous with *Troll-magic*

Winter Glory — 3 years after *Troll-magic*

A Talisman Arcane — 7 years after *Troll-magic*

J.M. Ney-Grimm lives with her husband and children in Virginia, just east of the Blue Ridge Mountains. She's learning about zero-carb eating, container gardening, and the discounted benefits of getting vitamin D from exposure to sunlight. The rest of the time she reads Robin McKinley, Diana Wynne Jones, and Lois McMaster Bujold, plays boardgames like Settlers of Catan, *rears her twins, and writes stories set in the magical realms of myth, fantasy, and the far future.*

Look for her novels and novellas at your favorite bookstore— online or on Main Street.

J.M. Ney-Grimm maintains a blog featuring flash fiction from her North-lands and other tidbits unearthed by her ever-active curiosity.

Visit her at http://jmney-grimm.com/.

www.ingramcontent.com/pod-product-compliance
Lightning Source LLC
Chambersburg PA
CBHW021116130626
46554CB00002B/720